TOMORROW IS ANOTHER DAY

TOMORROW IS ANOTHER DAY

NARMALA SHEWCHARAN

PEEPAL TREE

First published in Great Britain in 1994
Peepal Tree Books
17, King's Avenue
Leeds LS6 1QS
Yorkshire
England

© Narmala Shewcharan 1994

All rights reserved
No part of this publication
may be reproduced or transmitted
in any form without permission

ISBN 0 948833 47 5

To two wonderful people
— my parents —
With love

CHAPTER ONE

He opened the door cautiously, putting his nose through the crack as his eyes darted along the corridor. The noise in the outer office had subsided, but he wanted to be certain no one was around when he made his exit. He bit his lip. He was not afraid, but he did not want to face another unpleasant scene. They had shouted 'cutthroat' after him when he came to get the last of his papers a few hours ago. He would not put it past them to do more than shout when he walked through the office again.

He had been careful. No one had known about his intentions. Not even Paul Bagat, his assistant, often referred to as his shadow, had an inkling about what was going on. Not until he had made the final move.

They were shocked. They should not have been. He was sure that they envied him because he was taking an opportunity they would have grasped had they the nerve to ignore the good opinion of their contemporaries.

He was young, unlike them. He could not stay with them, wallowing in the stale politics of yesteryear, revelling in exaggerated memories of past glories and clinging to ever dimmer expectations of future triumphs. He closed the door quietly. If only there was another way out. Perhaps he should go now. Go quickly and get it over with. Facing them was only part of it. He had made his decision a long time ago.

He picked up his newly-acquired briefcase and took one lingering look at the office which he had occupied for nearly ten years. The two chairs in the room had been moved to a far corner, placed on each other. They had moved in quickly to dissociate him from the office. The waste-basket seemed heavy with its burden of shredded paper, bits of which blew listlessly across the rough wood floor. He had come here bursting with ideas, believing that his energy would change things. He shook himself impatiently. It all looked barren, alien. People were starving while they were playing with politics.

He put his hand on the knob. But someone was already turning it. He stepped back warily. It was Dada. He wished he was long gone or that he had never made this last journey. He braced himself for the recriminations.

Dada closed the door softly. His silver hair gleamed in the sharp beam of sunlight let in by the half-opened window. At seventy, his idealistic face retained traces of his good looks, but now his voice was weary. 'Jagru,' he said, 'I know you have to go because you are even more of a fool than I am. Here you're protected. Out there you'll be among wolves. We play a part. Even when they wish us in hell, they still allow us to play a part. But think what will happen when your role is no longer important to them.'

'Dada,' Jagru began uncertainly, but the older man ignored the gesture.

'I came to tell you to have a good time up there. We'll no doubt see each other in the 'big zoo' they call the House, as jokers on the opposite side of the fence, if nothing else. Come, I'll walk you the door.'

Jagru picked up his briefcase and followed him. The subdued chatter subsided as he entered the outer office. He tensed at the thought that there was going to be a long speech, but everyone was suddenly busy. He saw Dada shorten his stride, then stop and raise his hand to command their attention.

'Wish Mr. Jagru Persaud goodbye,' he told the staff.

Someone laughed unpleasantly. He did not look around, but felt instinctively that it had come from Sandra, the woman at the switchboard. They had been good friends a long time ago, but Sandra had mistaken the depth of their friendship and had read more into their casual dates. He knew that she had deeply resented his marriage. But it was not only Sandra who was hostile to him now.

These people had been his friends. In his enthusiasm to get away, to start anew, he had never realised how hard it would be to cut the ties, how deep the wounds would burn. Now he flushed with embarrassment, as he caught the barbed whispers and the sudden chorus of goodbyes.

'Don't forget us when you're a big one.' This came from Paul Bagat. He had tried to justify his action to Paul, but had made no headway. Paul had bitterly accused him of wanting company in his treachery.

Wiping the beads of sweat dripping down his face with the back of his hand, he darted for the door. He would forgive them the malicious laughter which followed him down the stairs. Perhaps they would understand one day, perhaps never understand. He was doing the right thing, could brave any amount of derision. But had it been worth risking their scorn to collect the file he had left behind? Perhaps it hadn't really been that important. But even as his mind whispered the words, he knew that he had not wanted to leave any documents behind. He had made enemies. He knew they would not forget.

A cool breeze rushed at his cheeks as he emerged from the building. It was the end of a chapter. One which had determined his life in many ways. But he would not allow sentiment to blind his path. He must forge ahead and go with a fresh mind and new ideas to his new colleagues. Go to the meeting which was being held today, solely, he believed, for his benefit.

But he had put off leaving until too late and now he was caught up in the rush period. Hundreds of people were converging from various directions. Getting a car to take him to his meeting would be difficult.

He walked out onto the road. The possibility always existed that someone would come rushing out from one of the dark alleys, looking for an easy victim. He was too well dressed. His eyes fell on a man lying on the pavement, scantily-clad and frothing. He glanced away, feeling imposed upon. Why wasn't he in hospital? But the thought had to be banished. There were many like him lying on the streets.

Too late he saw a coconut vendor jabbing savagely at the head of a green coconut and the water spurted out, drops splashing him. A young couple stood by, waiting for the juice, their serene contentment with each other clothing the day with happy illusions. He wanted to break in and destroy their daydreams.

He dragged his attention away from them. He must formulate his thoughts. He might have to make an address. Maybe they would just talk with him in a conversational way, but he should be prepared. He almost bumped into a fat woman who suddenly waddled in front of him to pick up a paper bag blowing down the road. She was selling peanuts at the corner. She broke into grumbling references to his new suit and his shiny briefcase. He muttered an apology, knowing that she was quite capable of launching a tirade against him to ease her own frustrations over low sales or some other trial.

He hurried towards the main street. There was no available car in sight. Each passing hire car had six or seven passengers crammed into it. He despaired of getting to the meeting on time. He began to walk hurriedly toward the car park after unsuccessfully trying to stop vehicles going the other way, with the intention of paying them double fare. If the drivers were willing to stop, he would go with the passengers already in the car and pay for that ride as well as the one he wanted to make. But even this ploy did not work. Maybe the time had come for him to buy a car. He could not even have entertained the idea before; such extravagances were frowned upon. His new colleagues at the Official Party would understand, he was sure, that he would have to get some mode of transport. But there were so many problems connected with the maintenance of a car. Fuel was not the least of the problems. He'd have to think about it. Maybe he could afford it. He still had some of the land his grandmother had willed him.

He had arrived at the car park, the scene of even worse chaos. Hundreds of people were standing, seemingly on the verge of riot, stampeding vehicles as their drivers steered into the park. This was impossible. He moved toward the special hire park, where the price was exorbitant, but the service reliable. Furtively, he checked the money in his pocket. Here at least the scene was relatively calm.

His mind was on his new job. He hoped they would give it to him immediately. That had been the offer. The job, then other things later.

As he got into the 'special car' he wondered about telling the driver to take a few of the others who were going his way, but did not voice this prompting. The driver would think he was just trying to share the price of the cab. And he was already late. The trip was only about three miles, but the man demanded $50. Then there would be the tip, despite the 'no tipping' practice. His thoughts were sour as he put the last few dollars back in his pocket.

The meeting should have started already. But when he got to the conference room, it was deserted. He sat down, putting his briefcase at the foot of the long table. Several minutes elapsed. He felt foolish. He got up and walked outside. He could see no one. He walked to the other end of the room which seemed to lead to an inner chamber. He thought he detected a murmur of conversation. He knocked tentatively. Nothing. He thought that he should feel angry. After all he was only a few minutes late. He went outside again, needing the fresh air. He stood in front of one of the new-looking benches, undecided whether to risk what was sure to be wet paint. He cocked his ear. A car was coming into the drive. A new Mercedes. The engine purred unobtrusively as it came into sight. He schooled his expression into seriousness. A sound behind him. Footsteps. He turned unhurriedly.

James Mitchell, one of the men he had met earlier, beamed at him and clapped him on the back. 'Eh, eh Persaud,' he said heartily, 'I didn't know you were out here. Man, you early. The meeting's not starting for another half hour yet.'

'But I thought it was supposed to start already,' Jagru protested.

'They put it off, man. One of the big boys coming and they have to wait for him.'

Jagru thought of his $50 but crushed a sharp retort. Which big boy was coming? Was it because of him? He felt a little excited. They were definitely interested. He had never doubted. He had timed his approach to them nicely, but it was so easy to overestimate.

Other cars began to arrive. Men in smart tie-dye shirt-jacs stepped out, holding straw-woven briefcases in their hands. He made a mental note as he looked at his own leather brief case. Most of them knew him and had heard of his joining their Party. They did not speak of this, but of commonplace things. One asked Jagru if he had picked up his card for foodstuff.

'What foodstuff,' he asked.

'Oh, you know — anything. Like butter, oil, milk,' the man replied vaguely. 'You know, the "State Coms." buy it from the stores and sell it back to the workers at the registered price. Stops blackmarketing that way.'

He had not picked up his card yet.

Another man was speaking in a low voice about a food item which had been banned, but which was openly being sold on the streets. He heard the words 'border' and 'share'. He affected not to listen. The talk ended as another car arrived. They watched silently as a man stepped out. Jagru knew that he was a minister and that his functions were many. He felt an excited fluttering in his heart.

The Minister strode towards them, greeting everyone boisterously, slapping a shoulder here, making a crude joke to another about some woman.

Jagru struggled to keep his expression impassive. The man was indelicate, but as the Minister kept talking to the others and had evidently not noticed him, he began to feel uncomfortable. Had he been wise to capitulate so quickly, with so little bargaining? Perhaps he shouldn't have made the first move, in the certainty that eventually he would have been approached. But after he had made the decision, he had not wanted to wait. Now, he squirmed uneasily until the Minister, after what seemed an unendurable time, turned to him.

'Glad you've decided to join us, Persaud,' he boomed. 'This country needs young men like you. Together we can build a self-sufficient land.'

Jagru shook the hand he extended, smiling stupidly.

Everyone went into the conference room and stood waiting until the Minister had seated himself. He waved them permission to do so. Jagru was introduced again. The business proceeded to reports on various projects. Jagru listened carefully. He felt that statements were being made for his benefit. He itched to ask about his duties, but kept silent. He had been asked to report to the Secretariat, but that was all.

When the meeting was over, the Minister beckoned to him to remain. There would be a rally at the Square in a few days' time. They wanted him there as a member of the Official Party. Jagru felt disappointed. He had not expected anything to happen immediately, but still he felt let down. He thought of Victor Ram Singh who had left the old Party like himself and within a week had become a Minister. Had he timed it wrong? No, he had not been wrong to leave. He could not have stayed with them any longer. He had grown beyond them.

Someone offered him a lift, but he refused. His home was not very far away and a walk would allow him to think. He knew the next few days would see an announcement in the papers. He might even be expected to speak at the rally. He would be happy to do that. It would give them another chance to evaluate him, to understand his value. He would speak on the rights of workers. He had always been able to speak eloquently on their struggles, and in truth he believed in that cause and had struggled for it for a long time, not always hopelessly. Now he was simply going about the struggle in a different way. He had not defected. Not from what was just and right, not from his beliefs. He had simply made a timely recognition of the influence wielded by those in power. He did not believe that one man alone was responsible for everything as the opposition claimed. There was, in reality, a complex power structure in which quite a number of people and groups had a share of authority and responsibility. He thought of the many things he could do with such authority — the many good things — and once again he was convinced that he had taken the right step. He would work his way through. He would make things happen. It would not be long before he was sitting in the right seat and being able to make an important contribution for the benefit of his fellow men.

★ ★ ★ ★

The faces were all alike, their empty, staring eyes making the rows of beds seem like a multiplication exercise designed solely to keep the women in white occupied. They were busy now, their white uniforms flitting among the columns, handing out bottles and issuing crisp instructions, as if their forced brightness could create the world they thought they wanted.

At the top of the stairs, Chandini Panday watched, waiting for their official sanction, the basket in her hand growing heavy. Her eyes searched the beds, seeing a little of her husband's face in each occupant, until the disembodied images joined to focus on a thin middle-aged man humped before the wall. She had a memory of another face. His, yet not his anymore, one that had sought challenges like a new day, one that belonged to some other existence. Chandi clutched at the memory, but before she could pin it down, the bell was ringing and the crowd behind her pushing and jostling to get into the wards. She allowed herself to move with their impetus, then suddenly found her anonymity withdrawn, as she moved towards the still figure seemingly engrossed in watching the wall. As if from afar, she heard sounds of greeting, mundane talk of household matters and sudden laughter. She sat awkwardly on the edge of the bed, waiting for him to acknowledge her presence.

He did not move. Chandi thought of the bills awaiting her at home, of the gold chain she had sold that morning. They would not keep his job forever. What could she talk to him about now? He had shut his eyes to her and the children. He had sought refuge in the hospital bed. She thought of the long hours she had put in earlier, knocking at the doors of offices, asking for work. She needed to find a job, if he was going to continue to sit there, staring into space.

The silence stretched the hour between them. When the bell was rung, he still had not finished his contemplation of the wall, using it as a barrier to her unspoken demands. She turned to go, picking up the basket from where she had placed it earlier. Then from a distance, she heard his voice.

'Chandi...' he struggled with the words, 'tomorrow ...' The effort seemed to exhaust him and he sank back into silence, renewing his contemplation with new intensity.

The hope which for a moment surged through her body was instantly replaced by anxiety. What did he mean? Would he tell them, the people in white, that tomorrow he was better? That he was ready to leave this sickness of the soul behind, take his job again and make haste to provide for his family? Or would tomorrow bring new pains, different indignities? It was time to go. The brief hope which had flickered would not even gain a place in memory; Chandi's thoughts had already shifted from the hospital bed to her enforced responsibilities.

She moved quickly down the street, trying to make

longer steps than her small frame allowed. Soon it would be dark and she wanted to get home, to be with the children. Home? She laughed mirthlessly. She had been dispossessed of the home she had helped to build for so many years with her husband, Lal. Then the marriage itself had seemed to disappear overnight, leaving her alone with the burden of all the tomorrows which came. All because of this sudden sickness. What was wrong with him? She glanced up at a nearby house, bright with lights. She realised that she was looking at the home of Radika, her old school friend. She had met them in town today: Radika and her mother-in-law, Kunti. She had helped them out by queuing for them in one of the food lines. She had told them her story. They had seemed sympathetic. She hungered for listeners and for their easy words of sympathy, but she stilled an impulse to go and knock at their door. She could not afford the luxury.

She walked on, quickening her pace. Soon, she found herself on the outskirts of the 'better areas' and moving toward the little shack in which she and her children had been forced to live. She saw her eldest daughter, Artie, standing in the makeshift doorway, waiting anxiously to greet her. She shook her head automatically in response to Artie's unspoken question. She did not want to raise false hopes, to tell Artie that he had at last spoken to her, had at last seemed to acknowledge that he was in the land of the living. He could have meant anything by his utterance of 'tomorrow'.

Artie began to cry. Chandi pressed her daughter to her bosom, telling her that things would change. She did not see how they could. Things were getting worse, but she could not break down. There was a huge flood inside her. She wished she could just let go, but she could not. Not while her children were putting their faith in her not to forsake them too.

Darkness had fallen. In the little shack, there would be no artificial glare of electric lights. There was no electricity, despite Chandi's repeated efforts to persuade the electric company to service the area. She had to cook outside the shack on an earthen fireside, fuelled by the driftwood the children had collected from around the neighbourhood. Now Artie busied herself, lighting the fire and preparing the meal. Chandi sat nearby, rocking herself on one of the few chairs which remained. The other children were still out and she watched the road, listening for sounds that would herald their return.

The moon was full and the flames from the fireside illuminated a wide circle around the place. Chandi realised it was bright enough to read, even to write after all. She got up abruptly and hurried into the shack. She rummaged in a barrel, seizing a little tin box. This contained her diary, one she had cherished when she was still a schoolgirl, dreaming of attending college and going on to a glorious career. Brushing away the dust, she flicked the pages open and stared at them for a long time. Who was that girl who had written those girlish things so long ago? There were still some empty pages, but what could this person she had become write now? She had moved so quickly from student to wife to mother that the diary, along with the other fripperies of her youth, had been flung aside. Now she felt an overwhelming need to put into words the despair thrust upon her since her husband had gone into hospital.

She sat still for a moment, then began: 'I don't know what to do. I just don't. I have no one to help me. No one.' She paused. The words, illuminated by the bright flames, seemed to magnify all her desperation and frustration. Her shoulders began to shake. Tears coursed down her cheeks and she began to cry with a wholeheartedness and an intensity that shocked her.

★   ★   ★   ★

His wife was sitting on the sofa. Her hands busily flicked the knitting needles back and forth. She did not look up, but held her body with an accusing stiffness. For a long time she had greeted him this way, expecting him to make the first, conciliatory move. But he would not appease her. It was she who had given birth to the first suspicions, vesting him with illicit desires and the ability to carry them out, a husband whose wedding anniversaries had grown heavy on him.

No. He would not tell her she suffered from delusions, as he once might have done. But that was in the days when he still remembered the vows he had taken and the fact that it was he who had pursued her. He had a sudden glimpse of a young and beautiful girl before the staleness of custom chased away the vision. He had married a Radika whom he thought believed in him and his ideals. In those early days she had always wanted to know about the things he wanted to do. He had thought that together they could conquer worlds. Where had this embittered woman, who seemed to be constantly contesting him in a battle of wills, come from?

Jagru wandered around the living room. The knitting needles clicked without pause. He felt awkward, like a stranger who is yet to be made welcome.

The room was comfortably furnished. The floor was highly polished, lace curtains bedecked the windows. She lavishes affection on the house, he thought. He sat down, watching her, wondering if he should tell her. She looked up, finally, breaking the studied concentration on her knitting.

'It's late,' she observed.

He nodded, then said: 'Yes.'

'Would you like to eat now?'

He nodded again, wearily, this time.

The eager questions about his work, the sensible suggestions did not come. She hugged her ill-concealed suspicions to her like a newly-born babe.

His mother, Kunti, came into the room. 'The children sleeping,' she gestured to an obscure end of the house, telling him what he had already guessed.

His wife rose and moved heavily towards the kitchen.

'Ma,' he said, 'I done it.'

His mother was silent for a moment, then she said: 'You done what you had to do, son.'

For a moment his burden felt lighter, then his shoulders slumped again. He knew his mother would always support him publicly. He knew, too, what she had left unsaid, the words she might have rebuked him with had she not been such a mother. *Your father would never have done it, would never have left one party for another.*

Jagru had spoken to Kunti about his intentions, told her what he wanted to do, outlined his motives before he took the step. It was a matter of survival to do what he had done. He had a right to be among those who made the decisions. He owed the right to his own kind and to all those others who suffered, who knew what it was like to begin life with defeat and failure grinning up front. If he was up there he would be able to make an impact, a difference, even if it was only a small one.

'Tell her yet?' his mother asked.

He shook his head.

'She knows.'

'She couldn't,' he said almost angrily. He had made up his mind that he would tell her nothing. Let her read it in the newspapers. Once, she had read the papers avidly; in the beginning she had even made notes, pointing out to him things that could not be. She didn't do that anymore. Perhaps she had felt that the words gained credibility by her constant perusal. But how could she know that he had left his old party and joined the Official one. Only his mother had known and she would have kept his confidence. He voiced the question.

'That man from the office. The one with the beard who used to come here sometimes. He was here earlier. He brought some books. He said they were yours. He told her. He said you were a 'cutthroat'. I ordered him from the house,' she added with remembered satisfaction.

Paul Bagat, he thought, lately his friend. Suddenly, he saw the isolation which would come with the new future, the past severed, some of his former friends not just angry, but storing up a vindictive hatred for him.

Outside the downpour had stopped as suddenly as it had started. Jagru shivered.

Radika came back into the room carrying a tray with a steaming bowl. He smelled onions and garlic; his tongue became moist. He realised that he was hungry and went to sit at the small dining table where, silently, his wife placed the bowl before him.

'You had dinner, Ma?'

Kunti nodded. His wife moved mechanically, arranging the bowl on the table. She, he knew, always managed to eat earlier or later than he. They had not sat down for a meal together for a long time. He ate quickly, almost greedily, enjoying the soup. She brought another dish before him, rice and stewed meat. He looked at the rice. It was the better quality. Where had they got it?

His mother anticipated him. 'Good rice,' she said; 'they were selling it downtown today. The line was not so long too.'

The food assumed a new dimension. 'You were in the line?' he asked. 'You not Radika?'

'Nothing wrong with me, son.' She showed him her arms. 'I strong and healthy. Radika was in another line, looking for oil,' she added placatingly. 'And I had help from Chandi. You remember Chandi. Poor thing. She husband in hospital and she with all those children.'

Chandi who? He did not want to hear about any Chandi. He pushed the food away. He could not bear the thought of his mother in the line. Last week, a woman had died in the line. She had been younger than his mother. There were other stories of women falling in the streets and being ignored. He remembered the naked man he had seen on the pavement earlier in the day.

'I'm strong,' his mother repeated. 'Eat your food.'

He found that all his appetite had gone. 'I'm not hungry. Ma,' he said earnestly, 'don't go joining lines. They rough sometimes out there.'

She wagged her fingers at him: 'How much you think you earning, son. We can't waste the money for blackmarket things all the time. If we don't join the lines, how we going to get to eat.'

'But you mustn't go, not you. Times are changing, you know, Ma. I have a better job, better pay.'

'You not thinking straight, Jagru boy. A lot of old women like me out there. And you know, I had help from Chandi, too.'

His wife reentered the room. Her suspicious gaze moved from mother to son, but as she heard the word 'Chandi', the lines in her face relaxed. She would not be jealous of that old hag who had more problems than she could count. She, unlike her old schoolfriend, had preserved her looks. No, Radika knew whom she could blame her problems on. Her lips pursed, she resumed her knitting, ignoring the food he had left almost untouched. If he didn't want to eat that was his business.

Jagru itched to say something nasty to her. He was furious that she had allowed his mother to join the lines. She had worked hard all her life, bringing him up single-handedly after his father had died. He knew that her back still ached with the constant bending she had done in the canefields and her hands were scarred from handling the long stalks. When he had made his mother retire from the fields, he had promised her comfort and told her she would never have to work again.

'Radika,' he began, his voice trembling with anger.

His mother, suspecting his intent, interrupted him. 'You worrying about nothing, Jagru,' she said, 'nothing.'

He did not answer. The silence lengthened. His thoughts turned to his new job. It was certain to pay more and he would soon know how much. He remembered the talk about the card. He would have access to foodstuffs, all the things they couldn't get at the moment. His mother wouldn't have to stand in the line again. He felt a sweet pleasure in the thought of this unlooked-for benefit which had come his way by switching parties. He turned to tell his mother, then thought better of it. He would wait until he had the card in his hands. He would surprise them with the bag of foodstuff. He was savouring the thought when his mother asked:

'So what post they give you? The man with the beard said they going to make you a minister.'

They were kind to him, he thought, to assume so much so quickly. 'Tomorrow,' he told his mother. He would know more tomorrow. He looked at his wife. 'Aren't you going to ask what we're talking about?' he demanded, playing with her.

She gave him an icy stare.

'But then you know already.' His voice was raised, betrayed into anger.

Radika shrugged her shoulders.

She would say nothing. His wife, the monument of silence. He felt stifled in the heat of his emotions. He would go for a walk. Another one. And later he'd drop in at Manu's. Manu. He still had to tell them. But they didn't care much about politics and the running of the country and suffered his presence because of that.

'Going over to Manu's place,' he said, averting his eyes from Radika. He did not want any further confrontation.

A fly circled the food on the table, buzzing intensely. Radika got up and attempted to swat it. She missed. He waited to see if she would object. She did not speak. She was thinking of Asha. The thought came to him suddenly and crystallised into certainty. She had nurtured her suspicions with nameless faces, until one day, she had settled for Asha. *She* was pretty, with a vivacity Radika once might have had. When she had hurled the accusation at him — in those days when she had not considered silence a weapon — he had said nothing, liking the idea. Did she think that he was going to see Asha now, that he was going to share his news with her? Did she think that was why he frequented Manu's place so much?

His mother said: 'You be careful on the road. The radio said some more of those jail men is out. They got one this morning. They shot him while he trying to escape.'

Jagru was not afraid to walk the streets at night, though he never went out with a watch or any jewellery. He had long ago stopped wearing his wedding ring — there had been a time when he himself had suspected Radika, an idle suspicion to counter his own growing dissatisfactions. He had left the ring in the bedroom and it had disappeared after that. He wondered where Radika had hidden it. She would have done it to punish him for something of which she had found him guilty.

He decided not to change out of the clothes he had specially purchased for the day. He wanted Manu and the others to see him in his new role, to see him as someone who was already important. He told his mother not to stay up, that she must have really tired herself and she should get some rest. Radika could draw her own conclusions.

As he was about to leave, remembering he had not locked his briefcase, he fished for the key in his pocket, locked it and put it in place behind the sofa. He moved towards the door. The clicking of needles followed him.

At Manu's, the lights were bright. The two brothers greeted him effusively. A child was playing the stereo. In another corner, two others were carrying on a lively conversation. Snatches of 'kung fu' and 'snakefist' drifted across to him. He guessed that they were talking about the Chinese film playing at a nearby cinema. Manu was talking about what he called another 'raid'. Jagru cocked his head attentively, but was thinking about himself, about what the next day would bring.

'They killed her afterward. The police find her with her hands tied. She had marks all over her body.'

The words pierced through Jagru's self-absorption. He stared at Manu. What was he talking about?

Manu shook his head sadly: 'Things getting worse. They take you gun. But what happens? They put these satellites overhead and everybody getting TV sense. They have more kickdown door bandits here than in the movies.'

Manu's brother, Bulu said: 'They nearly killed the bride at that wedding in Coconut Grove the other day, too. But the girl sensible. She take off her jewels and hand it over to them.'

Jagru sipped at the drink he had poured himself. 'Weddings going out of style,' he contributed. 'Nobody wants the police prying in their pots to see what contraband they're using to feed the guests.' He stopped. He remembered his new role. He should tell them now, before they thought that he had come to spy on them. But they could not think that.

Bulu was talking about what had happened at the market the day before. Wanton waste. His friend, Chuck, a candy vendor, was selling at a street corner where he should not have been selling. He had been too slow to move with his heavy basket when the men came, with their accusations that he had contraband in his stock. They had run after him, caught him, taken his candy away and destroyed it with their feet. Chuck had sat down on the street and cried like a little baby. Nobody had been sure who the men were. They had acted as if they had authority and certainly no one stopped to dispute their right to do what they had done.

'Beasts,' Bulu spat the words out, 'real hogs. Why did they have to do that when people starving all around them?'

Jagru was used to Bulu and Manu speaking in this way, but now he felt that he was in a false position. He should tell them now.

'I've left the party.'

The words did not register. Manu was scolding the child playing the stereo. 'You not see that needle sticking, Son-Son.' Bulu was busy filling his glass.

'I've changed parties,' he said more loudly this time.

'You going partying?' Bulu asked blankly.

'No,' he said patiently, 'I'm talking about my party, about

the United Party,' he explained immediately realising that it was not his party anymore.

'What happened to the United Party? They finally decide on some action?' This was from Manu who had finished his shouting.

'I've left them,' he said.

The two men stared at him with interest.

'Finished with them,' he added unnecessarily.

'Shoulda left them long time ago,' Manu said.

'But what you going do now?' Bulu asked. 'Want to join us?'

Jagru flushed. He should have told them immediately. 'I'm with the Secretariat now,' he mumbled. He felt the silence grow uncomfortable. The stereo had stopped playing and the voices of the children seemed to come from far away. He heard a door bang.

'So you with them now,' Manu said slowly.

Someone shouted from the hallway. It was Asha. He knew her voice, even her footsteps. He felt a gladness within him. He had sat there watching and listening — talking with the men — but all the time wondering where she was, though he never liked to ask, to betray any interest.

'Manu,' Asha was saying, 'give me some money to pay the taxi man. I tell you these taxi men are something else. If you're coming from the airport with more than three suitcases, they think you're loaded with money.'

Manu left the room with her.

Bulu asked him: 'You join the Official Party already, man?'

He nodded.

'They going to make you a minister,' Bulu pressed.

He shrugged.

'You had a big job in the U.P.. They should be glad to get you.'

'I've only just gone over. Tomorrow they'll probably tell me what I'm going to do.'

Bulu considered this in silence.

Asha came bursting into the room. She struggled with one suitcase. Manu had the other two in his hands. 'Thought I was never going to get here,' she said, plonking herself on a sofa. The children came running around her. She opened a small red bag which had earlier hung on her shoulders, matching her dress.

Red suited her, he thought, as he watched her.

She took out chocolates and sweets and distributed them.

Manu, after a sharp glance at Jagru, had opened one of the suitcases. In it were over fifty pairs of shoes.

'I got everything except the shoes at a reasonable price,' Asha said relaxing.

Bulu said: 'Asha, Jagru with the Secretariat, now.'

'Oh.' She had glanced at him briefly when she came in. Now she looked at him searchingly. 'Finally waking up?'

He smiled hesitantly.

'What are you doing?'

He explained again. 'It doesn't make a difference,' he added.

'What doesn't?'

'My being in the Secretariat. I mean what you do is your own business.'

'Of course, not,' she said. 'We've got our friends in the right places. But it will be nice to have another one.'

'We won't have to call you Mr. Minister, eh?' Manu asked, taking his cue from Asha's relaxed tone.

The children took up the chant in the corner: 'Mr. Minister. Mr. Minister.'

Manu spoke sharply to them.

'You won't have to call me anything,' Jagru rushed into

words. 'I'm not hungry for power. I'm just tired of seeing things go wrong. If I'm up there I may be able to help, even if it's just a little.'

'Man, it's your choice,' Bulu said. 'Personally, I would keep as far away as possible from that political jungle. It's better not to get involved. What's the use of licking asses. They can do what they want. Things couldn't be better.'

'For you maybe,' Jagru said, 'but what about all the others out there who don't have enough money to start even a little trading business.'

'That's the law of the jungle, Jagru,' Manu cut in. 'The strongest survive, and you better learn that where you're going. They have strong teeth up there.'

Asha said: 'When the man comes for the shoes, tell him the price is 5% more unless he takes the lot. I hear the currency dropping again. They hold up nearly everybody's goods at the airport. Good thing your friend was on duty. Man, I tell you, they have some real chicken hawks at that airport. You know one of those small boy gangs ran after my suitcases trying to lift it off the trolley. I soon told them where to go.'

'We promised our friend something next week,' Bulu observed.

Jagru fidgeted. They were talking business, personal things. But he did not want to go. Not yet.

Manu opened another of the suitcases. It contained an assortment of denim jeans. Jagru knew that these were expensive. The prices often ranged from $150 to $300. And many civil servants did not take home more than $350. He often wondered how people could afford such prices. He himself had started out as a store clerk at $17 a week in what was known as the 'cheap time'. That was before he had joined the United Party. He had worked at that job for nearly six months before he had got another with slightly better pay. Eventually, he had earned his degree in Economics and moved on to teaching, though this career was soon aborted because of his expanding interest in politics. In the U.P. he had earned just under $500 net. He started. Manu was talking to him.

'Nice, soft pair.' Manu waved a pair of shoes at him. 'Think they would fit your mother?'

Jagru held the shoes in his hands. They were soft. Ma would like these. But he would not be able to afford them. Not just yet. 'Too expensive, man.' He proffered the shoes to Manu who pushed them back to him.

'A present,' Manu said, 'from us. Tell your Ma.'

Jagru held the shoes in his hands. From time to time they had given him things for his mother. They liked the old lady. He laughed silently at himself. It was not a bribe. Why should they bribe him? He was still a nobody. He did not even know what his job was.

Asha was talking about a party. Her birthday. She insisted that Jagru must come and bring his wife and kids and his mother, of course. She would take his acceptance for granted. She was talking now about the airport, about the mad scene she had left behind her. People who could not find their bags. One woman who had arrived the previous day minus her bags had been walking about the airport in her nightgown, carrying on loudly.

Asha's face was animated as she told the story. He watched her fascinated. It was amazing the way she switched from topic to topic, grasped ideas and then threw them away.

Manu was repacking the suitcases. Bulu busied himself making an inventory.

He wondered how old she was. She often looked very

young, but she was older than Bulu, he knew, who was the youngest. He guessed her age to be around twenty-seven.

'You're not listening to me,' she accused him suddenly.

He protested. She had switched to the chaos at another airport, the country where she had gone to buy her goods, how they'd had to make a crazy dash for the plane and one woman had been left behind because there had been no seats left. There had been a terrible scene because the woman had a reservation and a seat number.

'She should sue the airline,' he said, to prove that he had been listening.

She dismissed the idea with a wave of her hand. 'Waste of time... Money down the drain.' She yawned. 'I think I'm going to turn in. It's been a long day.'

Jagru felt disappointed. He nearly asked her if she would be in tomorrow if he were to come, but he caught himself in time.

She was always flying in and out of the country, bringing back suitcases filled with assorted goods. He marvelled at her audacity. But then they had friends in the right places. Did these men get shoes for their mothers too? Maybe their girlfriends? The thought leapt into his mind and took root, but he knew that he was being foolish. The gift meant nothing.

He watched her go up the inner staircase. She walked like a gazelle even when she was tired. He experienced a sharp feeling which he could not identify immediately. Was it pain, desire, regret? He thought of his own wife, waiting for him at home. She would be pretending to be asleep when he came in.

It was getting late and he knew that if he sat there Manu would talk all night. He and his brother used talk as a way of letting out all the suppressed energy of things they could not do. The children had long since gone to bed. Two of them were Manu's and often proved a handful. Manu's wife was 'outside' the country, studying. Manu was talking about some currency deal. It was time to go.

As he left they urged him to stop by and tell them if anything broke.

Tomorrow was on his mind as he walked out into the night, gazing at the dark sky as if to find answers. He walked slowly, holding the parcel tightly under his arm. He wished he had left it behind, had collected it during the day. It was too attractive in its bulkiness. He looked around warily and saw a policeman in the distance, walking in slow, measured steps. He knew the man, had known him since he was a child. He felt a sudden pity. Creatures of the night, he thought, but could not tell whether the pity was for himself or the other.

He had done irrevocable things today, things that would make or break his life. He could not just go to bed and sleep it off. He turned around and began to retrace his steps. He looked up at the stars, making a haphazard count. Not many out tonight. The dark clouds had swallowed them.

He passed the policeman again. They exchanged a greeting and the policeman looked at him in a puzzled fashion. He decided not to go any further. What if there was a burglary? He would be remembered, walking late and walking aimlessly. He turned around and fell in with the policeman who began talking about cricket in a mournful voice, how it would always attract bad weather whenever they had a good match going.

Images flashed across Jagru's mind. He saw a younger version of the policeman, dressed in immaculate white, at the wicket, batting. The crowd was cheering. How much had the policeman scored? He searched his memory until he arrived home. All the while the policeman talked on in his mournful voice. The light was out in his bedroom. But there was one burning in the hall. She would not be asleep.

★ ★ ★ ★

Radika had been turning the matter over and over in her mind all afternoon and evening, trying to see a way out. How could he be so blind, so foolish? Couldn't he see that there was nothing here for them? Nothing good? She wanted to leave, to get out. She had hoped in time to persuade him to this way of thinking, despite her belief about his infidelities. Why couldn't he accept her mother's invitation? Everybody with any sense was leaving, although not everyone was so fortunate as to have a mother-in-law outside the country who was willing to help out. Why was he being so foolish, getting himself even more deeply involved in the mess? What was there in the stupid politics of the place which could be keeping him? There had to be something else, someone he was really serious about. She would show him that she didn't care anymore what he did. She would take her own steps.

CHAPTER TWO

Chandi hurried quickly into the electricity office. She was on her way to the hospital, but she had to make this stop and ask the people again when they were going to give her lights. She thought guiltily of the unpaid bills from the other house, but the demands of her children were greater, especially Das who was having great trouble studying by the light of the fire and the street lamp. But she was not allowed to go very far. They knew her by now and the guard was standing by the gate, demanding to know her business. Chandi reiterated her demand for lights. She felt the guard's eyes on her, dwelling on her old faded dress which had seen too many night-washings for next day's wear. '

'Nobody live in that place,' the guard said. 'Don't you know that is government land?'

'But we pay taxes, you know!' Chandi broke off abruptly and jerked herself away as she felt the hand of the guard caressing her shoulder.

'You a pretty woman,' the guard leered. 'What's you man doing to let you go begging like this. Why don't you let a proper man take care of you.'

'You're an animal,' she spat the words at him, walking away without looking back. She felt as if her face had been slapped, that he had been particularly insulting because anyone could see she was aging, that her lined face was showing every second of her thirty-eight years. What made it worse was the discovery she had made that morning. She was carrying a child. She had not wanted another. Five were too many, especially when the future loomed so dark. Already there were too many demands on the little cash she was able to get by selling her jewellery. It was not enough for the rent, not enough for Das' exams, not enough for the new school clothes which Janki needed. She had saved some money when Lal had been working in the sugar factory, but all that was gone, swallowed up in his strange illness.

She had to get Lal to listen to her, to stop shutting the world out and find out what was going on. What if they refused to keep his job open? She had to make him sit up and listen, to stop being a pale shadow on the bed, looking at the wall as if that was all there was to life.

'Under observation'. What did they mean by 'under observation'? How long would they keep a man 'under observation' without finding out what was wrong with him, without discharging him, telling him to go home and look after his children? She would tell him this time. She would hide it from him no longer that they had been kicked out of the house and were now living in a shack.

But before Chandi could open her mouth, Lal had grabbed the basket from her hand and began, with unaccustomed energy, to check the contents. Perhaps he was recovering, she thought hopefully.

'This food's no good, Chandi,' he said. 'You know I don't like food like this and it's badly prepared.'

Although the protest welled up inside her, she did not voice it; he was at least showing interest in things again. She buried the impulse to tell him that the money for the food had come from the sale of one of her bangles and that she had stood for hours in several food lines before she'd been able to get all the necessary items. Instead she waited to hear what next he had to say.

He looked at her sullenly: 'I leaving today. The doctors say the beds are filling.'

She felt glad, though she knew that they had told him to go because the money had run out to pay for the special attention which he seemed to want. She watched silently as he prepared his things to leave the hospital. His shoulders were slumped as if he had just been sentenced to jail, instead of being reprieved from his hospital bed. He looked terrible, but Chandi did not care. Her only thought was that she would no longer have to struggle alone, that her family was whole again, that her husband was coming home.

He took the news badly that they had been kicked out of their old home by the landlord's bailiff and were now living in a shack. He began to abuse her as if she were responsible, and though she could have told him that it was because he had taken all the money to pay the people at the hospital that there had been none left to pay the rent, she said nothing.

When he had finished abusing her, Lal began to threaten how he would give that 'fat-arsed' landlord a good thrashing.

Chandi pleaded with him. There were other, more important things, to do. The man who 'owned' the shack would soon be there to collect another $15 and they did not have much money left. She still had several pieces of jewellery, but decided she would not mention that.

Lal was incensed. 'Why you paying rent for government land?'

'But the shack isn't a government shack,' Chandi explained, 'and the man kind to give we this place when we had nowhere else to go.' She was almost crying now.

But Lal was shutting her out again. He had gone into the shack and was sitting down, staring in front of him.

Chandi's heart sank. She had to stir him into action.

'Your job's still there,' she told him. 'They said they would keep it open for another month.'

Lal turned a furious face to her. 'Why I go take back that job? You think I'm a machine to be cutting cane all my life? Eh? You ever try standing up for hours at the car park to get transportation, then bending your back for the rest of the day in a wet muddy field? They can keep their damned job. No more slave work!'

'But Lal, what we going to eat. How we going to live?'

'You manage all right without me when I was in hospital,' he flung at her, 'or you want to sit down in luxury all your life.'

He did not want to know. He brushed aside her entreaties. Did she call this existing? One could not just live to eat. Was this all life was about. 'There're things which a real man should do to maintain his dignity,' he told her. 'In this land it have only slaves and blasted parasites.'

Chandi had exhausted her pleas. This was not the man she had married, this stranger who did not seem to care whether she or her children lived or died. She felt tired, felt that she was only wasting her time, that he had shut his ears to her forever. She went slowly, heavily out of the shack.

Artie was standing by the fireside, a stricken look in her eyes. She had just arrived from school and was busying herself soaking the logs in kerosene so that they would burn easily. She had listened to the angry words between her parents and had divined correctly that her father's presence had changed nothing.

'Ma, what we going to do?'

Chandi said nothing. She went to sit in her chair and began to rock. Eventually, she said: 'Things going to be all right. Don't worry.' Artie was a good girl, with a strong mind to bear the adversities of life, but she did not want her to lose heart. Already, she was having trouble with Janki who, just a few years younger than Artie, seemed to want all kinds of fancy things to wear.

Her eldest son, Das, had arrived by this time. He seemed pleased to see his father at home, but after Artie told him what had occurred, he knocked his books down and ran to sit under a nearby tree. Chandi went to talk to him. She was determined that nothing would come between him and the education she wanted him to have. She remembered too well her own shattered dreams in that respect, because, even though her father was a schoolteacher, she had lived in a village where they did not believe in women wasting time on books.

'You mustn't mind your father,' she said to Das. 'People go through these changes in life. He'll soon come around back and become the father we've all known.'

'But Ma, why we have to live in this dump? They does buff us up at school when they hear where we living. Is Pa fault. Why he so weak. Why can't he stay strong like you? Is only women who are strong?'

Chandi hushed him. She knew that if Lal heard what his son was saying, there would be a beating.

Das was silent for a moment, then he said: 'Ma, I want to leave school. I can't bear to study when I see how you all suffering.' And then he added quietly, so that she only just caught his words: 'A man offered me a job today.'

Chandi was instantly alarmed. 'What kind of job?'

'A good job, good money. We wouldn't have to live in this shack anymore.'

'Das,' Chandi said, all her fears assuming reality, 'promise me you wouldn't take that job. I don't want you mixed up in smuggling. We going to make out somehow. Things going to change for the better. You'll see,' she gestured to the shack. 'He won't always be like this. Tomorrow I going to make him see things differently. Son, you have to promise me you forget this and keep in with you studies. You want to break my heart too?'

Hours after, when all the children had gone to sleep, she lay staring into the darkness, only a rice bag separating her back from the mud floor. She had given the children the two mattresses salvaged from the old house.

Lal had gone to sit outside, complaining about the heat. She thought she could hear him now, slapping mosquitoes and quarrelling with the night. She could not sleep, listening, she suddenly realised, to hear if his footsteps would carry him away from the shack.

Then she heard him come in. But before she could turn on her side and pretend a snore, he was already lying down on the mats she had prepared for him and was soon asleep. Chandi found that she could not lose her consciousness so easily. She thought about her children as she watched them sleep. Shyam, her youngest, whimpered and she reached out her hand to soothe his head. The girls were sleeping closely together, stretching the short sheet between them, their arms entwined. Das ground his teeth. She would have to talk to him again.

Das was the first to wake and she got up with him to prepare the breakfast, using the last of the plantains. Shyam had stopped asking for roti and Das and the girls never complained, though Chandi sometimes thought with shame that when Janki stayed out late, she ate at her friend's home.

Much later, after all the children had left for school, Lal emerged from the shack. He looked rested and had a spring in his step.

I have to go out,' he said. 'I meeting some important people.'

'How long you going to be, Lal?'

He shrugged.

'You expect me to carry on like this?'

He said nothing for a while, then said, 'You father helping out, na?'

'How can I ask he to help we? He give we plenty in the past, and the man old.'

Her father had long since stopped giving classes. She could not hurt him by letting him know just how badly-off she was. He imagined that she was living in a fairly comfortable way. It would be cruel to dispel this illusion.

'Lal, man, I sell off nearly all me jewellery. I have only a few piece left. What I go do next?'

'Sell the rest. What good they for? They just useless ornaments. Look, I going to help, but I can't do anything just yet. I going now.'

She could not let him go just like that. How was he going to help? But her head hurt and she didn't have the energy to resume the quarrel from last night. Instead she asked: 'If you not going back to the sugar factory, what about severance pay or whatever they call it?'

He shrugged his shoulders again. Before his 'illness' he had been a talkative man and she had often wearied of this trait. Now, she found his lack of communication frightening and she wanted to press him into words, to say anything, so that she could feel he was part of her world again. But he left without another word.

Chandi doubted that he would go to the sugar factory for any pay which might be due to him. When he had been in hospital, she had gone to them and had tried to get them to pay her some money for his illness. They had refused, saying that he was only playing the fool and that nothing was wrong with him. She wondered if she should go again and tell them this time that he was leaving the job. Would this be another waste of time? They wouldn't want to give her any money, but she couldn't just sit and wait, hoping he would come back with some. But where had he gone?

She went into the shack and began to dig at a corner of the mud floor where she had hidden a small bundle. She took out another piece of gold jewellery. She was glad now that her father had held such a big wedding for her and that so many of the presents had been jewels.

The last time she had gone to the market, the man had bickered with her, wanting to reduce the already meagre price. This time, she told herself as she hurried there, if he had anything to say, she would find another buyer. But to her surprise, she did not have to haggle with him and quickly completed the transaction to her satisfaction.

She returned to the shack to find a strange man and a woman with her husband, engaged in close conversation. He scowled at her and motioned that she must not sit too close to overhear. She wondered for a moment if these people had come to help, but their shabby appearances denied this and the snatches of words she overheard from the shack made her feel uneasy.

But when Lal came out of the shack he was smiling and the look on his face was relaxed. In response to Chandi's silent enquiry, he took out an envelope from his pocket and gave it to her.

'The money from the sugar factory. Make it last.'

She looked inside the envelope. Sixty dollars. What did he mean make it last?

'You get a new job?'

Lal was silent, seeming not to hear, then he replied: 'Yes, but don't go expecting money. There isn't going to be any money for a while.' Chandi stared at him uncomprehendingly, as he continued, 'I made a big decision today, Chandi. A decision for you, for me, for all the children. I've joined the Worker's Party, you see. I working as an organiser for them. We have to go back to headquarters.'

Chandi watched stupidly as he left. When the full import of his words reached her, she felt that everything was lost. He could not mean that he had become political. He could not mean that. She knew what happened to people who got mixed up in politics. She had heard too many stories of people who had been locked up or killed for opposing the Government. Lal liked to talk too much — and he was such a meagre, small man too. What would happen to her children? What would happen to her? She wanted to cry loudly and tear at her hair. Why was all this happening to her? What wrong had she done in her life? She prayed to God every day and every night. Where had she gone wrong?

After a while, Chandi calmed herself. She thought that she would go and visit Radika and her mother-in-law. She needed to be with people. She would go mad if she were left to her own imagination. She saw her husband locked up, her children scattered, she, perhaps, walking the streets, one of those people who had gone mad. She shuddered at the thought.

She set out on the road toward Radika's home. Kunti, if not Radika, would be sympathetic. Why had her old school-friend become so cold and remote? The last time she had gone there, Radika had hurried out of the house almost instantly, saying she had an appointment to keep. It was Kunti, Radika's mother-in-law, who had made her welcome and given her words of encouragement and hope. Now, as she knocked at the door, it was Kunti who was standing there, beaming a welcome.

'Radika out,' Kunti said, as she told her to come in. 'She out plenty these days.'

Chandi hardly listened to her. She was eager to unburden herself, to tell her story.

Kunti looked grave, disturbed and agreed with her that she needed to be careful, that if her husband was going to become too active, if he was going to stick his neck out, then she needed to keep a strong head. She promised to help if she could. She knew a woman at the market — Aunt Adee — who worked and slept there — she was almost an institution. Aunt Adee would know if there were any jobs going and might be able to help.

Chandi said she would go and see the woman immediately. Any job would be welcome. Kunti told her too about her son, Jagru, that he was a big man in the right place now and as soon as he settled in, he would be in a position to help her. Chandi felt cheered. She always did when she'd seen Kunti. Kunti had seen hard times and meant well.

★ ★ ★ ★

Chandi thought she'd never seen a stranger person than Aunt Adee. She was small and thin like a piece of bamboo stick, but she looked as fat as a circus woman because of the paper and plastic bags tied all over her body, even to her frizzled hair. Chandi was almost afraid to go and talk to her, but Aunt Adee had a kindly smile and soon she summoned the courage to approach.

Aunt Adee had a cheerful, philosophical way of talking; problems were an unknown species to be eradicated for their obscurity. Chandi soon found she was telling Aunt Adee her whole story. Aunt Adee told her not to worry. There was a cookshop inside the market which was hiring people. In fact, they always wanted people to work because the woman was so quarrelsome. Aunt Adee warned Chandi not to say she had sent her. The cookshop woman quarrelled with everybody.

It seemed to be true. As she approached, Chandi could hear the woman screaming at the top of her voice for the police. Customers were running out of the shop and a woman shouted out, 'The man naked!' When Chandi went into the shop the man who had caused the commotion was standing there with a bowl of food in his hand. His body was covered with dirt and Chandi had to look twice before she realised that he had no clothes on. His eyes could barely be seen through the grime. He could not have been more than twenty-five. There were so many like him — the growing band of deranged people walking the streets. Chandi felt chilled and shivered, as if someone was walking on her grave.

The cookshop woman was still screaming after the man who was walking slowly away. He could have the food, but she wanted her bowl back.

A cigarette vendor on a pitch opposite the cookshop called out, 'I don't know what this country coming to. They have more mad people outside than inside. Is time they stop holding meetings and start building more mad houses.'

The woman at the cookshop had by this time noticed Chandi's approach, stopped her shouting and adopted her most obsequious manner, in the mistaken belief that Chandi was a potential customer.

'Come, come. He just a mad man. He won't come back.' She did a pantomime of smiling and clasping her hands as she tried to urge Chandi to enter the cookshop.

Her manner underwent an immediate change when Chandi told her she had come about the job. She placed her hands on her hips, demanding: 'You could cook?'

'I've never done anything else in my life,' Chandi said. She was not going to tell the woman that she was the daughter of a schoolteacher; that might make her even more hostile.

The woman snorted. This was what the last girl had said, but she had burnt everything in sight and wanted to sit down all the time. The girl never spoke nicely to customers and had all sorts of people coming in to meet her during working hours. 'You have anybody coming to meet you?'

'I'm married, ma'm, and my husband, he working, he don't have time to come around.'

The woman looked at Chandi's left hand, then questioned her further. Chandi told her that she came from over the river, but now lived in town, that her home was only 15 minutes away.

'You can have the job,' the woman said at last, 'but only on trial. We go see what *you* burn.' The pay was $35 a week. With meals that was a lot, the woman insisted. Chandi knew that the pay was poor, but the food would make up for it.

At first she felt pleased how easily she had got the job, but she soon realised why. The workload was staggering. Madam was preparing for the two o'clock rush and Chandi was to be the cook, the maid and general factotum. The sink was filled with dishes. There were basins of fish and shrimp to be prepared. The place was small and it smelt; a nearby garbage can had spilled over, attracting dozens of flies.

Chandi didn't know how she got through the day — so many things to do and all to be done at once. She was constantly rushing back and forth in attempts to split herself between the numerous tasks.

In the presence of customers the owner would hug Chandi and praise her cooking, but when they were on there own, there was a snarling, tough edge to her voice.

Chandi's thoughts were on her children as her hands mechanically carried out the tasks. She did not think of her husband. It was the road to madness to wonder what he might be doing; it was better not to know.

At the end of the day, the cookshop woman gave her a generous portion of food to take home with her, though Chandi knew that this was not inspired by any altruistic motive. The food would just have spoilt if it had been left until the next day, because the cookshop had no refrigerator.

Chandi hailed Aunt Adee as she went by, wishing she had something to give her to show her gratitude. Aunt Adee shook her head. She did not want anything, but she had more tips to give Chandi. She and her children could hire themselves out to the food lines on Saturday. There were often people who did not have the time to stand in the lines and they paid professional 'liners' to do the job for them. They only paid a dollar, but it added up to quite a few dollars before the day was done. Chandi nodded. She and her children would come on Saturday. Aunt Adee also told her that when she managed to save a little money, she could leave the cookshop job and sell outside the market. She would need a little capital, not only to purchase the goods, but also to give to the market constables and the people who were selling near to her so, that they would not give her a hard time and dispute her right to her selling spot. Chandi clasped the woman in a sudden hug. She was a stranger and looked so odd, but was being so kind to her.

When she reached home, she could see Das sitting under his tree, staring into space and scowling. The other children were huddled together, not talking, but just sitting. *He* was inside the shack. *He* had papers spread all over the place, so that there was no space for anyone to go in.

Why did he have to bring his papers home she wondered in alarm. He was jeopardising all of them, all the efforts she was making. Why did he want to set up against the administration? He was entering a maze from which none of them would come out as themselves.

Had he forgotten that there were many tomorrows to come and that his children had to eat? She felt so tired. Her mind began to assume a strange calm. What was the use? It could only end one way.

CHAPTER THREE

Jagru was euphoric. He had bumped into Asha on the way to work and they had exchanged friendly words. Now he thought of the way she had looked, the way she sounded, her gestures. He remembered all these with possessive detail. But she was not his, not in the way that Radika imagined. Yet in a curious sense, she belonged in the scheme of things. Just the fact that she was around excited him, though he shied away from putting his half-formed longings into any concrete form. She had always treated him warmly, had even from time to time expressed interest in his activities. When he had seen her just recently at Manu's she had seemed most interested in his new position. He fastened on the thought and worried it all the way to the Square, where he was heading to take part in the rally. Why her particular interest? It was flattering, but what did she mean by saying she thought him daring to have switched over to the Official Party. Had she lost respect for him? Perhaps she really didn't care one way or the other? Why was he getting in such a sweat over it anyway?

By now he had reached the Square and, with some trepidation, he went to take his official seat with his new colleagues, reluctantly abandoning his inner debate.

People had turned out at the rally in great force. The numerous school children present made him believe that all the schools in the city had been given official notice to turn out in full. Many of the children had flags in their hands and, overhead, banners flapped, as if agreeing with myriad colours which patterned the crowd.

He was still sweating and kept wiping his brow. Just a short while ago there had been chanting. Now the loudspeaker was silent. The chattering around him ceased almost simultaneously. The lively wind picked up a low hum from within the depths of the crowd and brought it to jangle with the silence. There were never such crowds at our rallies. He caught himself. This was his rally now. He must completely disassociate himself from the past. Whatever people said about the Official Party, you had to admire their organisation, the shows they put on.

He could hear sirens in the distance. The man who had been speaking earlier into the microphone got up. The policemen on their massive motorbikes came into view. A sleek, dark-coloured car followed. At the microphone, the man began to urge the crowd. People began to shout and clap and cheer. This was absurd. These people were suffering. Many could not afford proper food. He wanted to shout at them, to urge them not to glory in their suffering. Instead, he found that his own hands had somehow come together and that from his own throat came the sound of 'hallelujah' to echo the roar of the crowd.

P.M. Rouche had arrived. He was small and rumours of his ailing health preceded his appearance everywhere. But this counted for little against the feverish energy of the man at the microphone, who poured forth praise for the nation's achievements under Rouche.

The crowd was silent now, waiting.

P.M. Rouche looked very old, his dark skin seemingly encased in an unnatural whitish hue. According to the predictions and hopes of his critics, he should have been dead long ago, but he had managed to confound all the reports.

Years ago he had been a spry, energetic man of boundless enthusiasm who had pledged to the nation that he would make them a prosperous people and lift them out of the morass of colonial oppression and exploitation. He had made much of his own dark skin, ignoring totally the split roots of his own mixed descent and made awesome speeches about the proud continent from which his ancestors had been uprooted, bound in chains and dragged across an indifferent ocean into the horrors of slavery.

Rouche had won the support of *his own* people, as he liked to call them. His appeals had been directed at them in exclusive denial of the many other races which inhabited the land, including those whose forebears had come as indentured immigrants, driven by desperate poverty in India to sell their souls for five years and risk all for a chance of a better life. For a time, it seemed, he had even managed to persuade many of the other peoples, despite all the evidence to the contrary, that he could unite the people and had all their interests at heart. Whatever, when the election results were out, Rouche had won.

Inevitably there were whispers, muted ones, that he could not have won by fair means. But whispers they remained. The country had just passed through a time of fire and bloodshed provoked by unscrupulous politicians who had seen their chances in playing on racial tensions. No one wanted to risk another such outbreak, and so the pretender, who had done most to fuel the flames, had been allowed to keep his ill-gotten throne.

Over the years he had changed his style, if not the substance, of his rule, sensing that he could do much to defuse future threats if he could put together a government which had at least the semblance of representing all the races. But now it was all coming apart. There were too many ministries and too many state corporations filled with talentless party bureaucrats, and over the years productivity had declined and only corruption and inefficiency had grown. Now the white-corner mouth of hunger had made its reappearance in the land.

Once Rouche had been full of energy and bombast; now even that had deflated like a split balloon. He was an old man, an ailing man. Yet he still managed to keep the people cowed, to allow no more than whispers about the corruption of his Government. He was even managing to attract new blood into his party out of the opposition stable. Who could claim that his regime did not represent all the races when men like Jagru were on his platform, and the man at the microphone welcoming him boasted ancestors from Sicily?

But his energy was gone. Now, it seemed, he could not even feel that deep satisfaction which he had once derived from orchestrating the emotions of a huge crowd. He stirred uneasily in his seat, wanting to be back in the cool of his office, away from the heat and the constant gaze of the people, all wanting something. He allowed his gaze to move irritably around, alighting on the new man who had come up from the U.P.. Some of them, at least, were learning the lesson: that they would never be in his class, would always be followers.

Jagru sensed the P.M.'s scrutiny, but felt it would be unseemly to return his attention.

He scanned the paper which one of the organisers had given him. He had been pleased when they had placed the paper in his hands, thinking that he was considered important enough to merit a scriptwriter. Naive fool, he immediately chastised himself. They had given him a script because they wanted to be sure they knew what he was going to say. It was a brief speech. He would speak on the achievements of the Party. They laid claim to many things. He did not have to look to become familiar with the grandiose words. He had read many similar speeches in the papers.

Still, he felt a little nervous before the huge crowd and hoped that his voice would be strong when his time came to speak. He heard his name over the loudspeaker. Another burst of cheering from the crowd. He was immobilised for a moment.

Fools, he thought. What did they know of him that they should cheer in such a manner. Had they been so wound up as to cheer at any idiot that wanted to make a spectacle of himself? He found himself before the public address system. He felt the ministerial gazes upon him. The crowd, he thought, grew attentive. He was fresh. What new things would he have to offer them?

But as he read his speech, he heard the mechanical claps of approbation as he paused at the correct intervals. He was on the right side, he was saying the right things; they had heard it all before.

He returned to his seat, drained. He felt that he had put on a good performance. The P.M. was looking at him. There was a slight nod which he was obliged to acknowledge. His back was soaked.

Next to him, Mitchell nudged him. 'That was good, man,' he mouthed.

The programme was almost finished. Jagru stood up with the others for the freedom songs, the musical renditions and the solemn playing of the national anthem by the Police Band. The crowd remained standing, urged to a new burst of cheering by the man at the mike, as the sirens roared above the applause, clearing a path for the P.M.'s car.

Jagru remained on his feet, feeling awkward. He did not

quite understand the rules and did not know what to do next. Should he just go back to the Secretariat or did the ending of the rally signal other activities?

'Coming for lunch?' Mitchell asked.

'What lunch?'

'At the Secretariat,' Mitchell replied. 'You know they always give you lunch after these events.'

He had not known. He crammed into the car Mitchell was driving, along with several others. It was the Secretariat's car, but Jagru had discovered that Mitchell always had it and even took it home at night. He began to wonder whether he might not need to go the expense of buying a car, that his new job might provide him with one.

He sat in uncomfortable closeness with the others as they waited for the crowd to thin. People were streaming in all directions and several traffic officers were on the streets trying to bring order to the situation. Finally, Mitchell was able to manoeuvre the car out of the Square.

Another crowd was at the Secretariat's canteen — mainly workers from the various outlying departments. Jagru collected a lunch box for himself. Some of the people greeted him by name, but most were too busy eating to register his presence. He took the box to a table in the corner where Mitchell joined him. He watched as Mitchell opened his box and began to eat hungrily.

'You not eating, man?' Mitchell asked, his mouth full.

Jagru opened his box. He took a fork and began to play with the chicken. More people came into the canteen. Mitchell was telling him about some films they were going to show later. That was another thing they always did. Show documentaries. Abruptly he asked: 'Mitchell, what am I supposed to do?'

The other man paused with his fork in the air. 'Why do

you want to do anything? They've given you a letter about your salary, haven't they?'

The personnel department had indeed sent him a letter, confirming his position as an Officer Grade II, whatever that was, quoting a huge salary with several superfluous allowances. But he did not know what he was supposed to do and he had been unable to get any sense out of personnel on the matter.

'I mean my duties.'

'What do you think *I* do?' Mitchell asked.

Jagru said nothing.

'Relax, enjoy life. When they want you to do something, they'll tell you.' He went back to his eating.

Jagru continued to toy with his food. Would they really let him sit there and do nothing? Did they all do nothing? But that was a different kind of nothing. The nothing they did was connected to power. He could not sit here and do nothing. It would soon be forgotten that he had come to them from the other party. It was not as if he was unskilled, uneducated. He was a veteran politician. His mother had spent many years bending in the canefields to give him a reasonable education. He had made many sacrifices to get his degree in Economics through part-time study. He threw the box away and returned with Mitchell to the main room. There he found the desk which they had shown him on his first visit. On it was the latest newspaper. He picked it up and scanned it eagerly, hoping that, finally, they would mention his appointment. He found the paragraph on one of the inside pages. It, too, did not say what he was going to do. His disappointment mounted.

At a nearby desk, a man who had been introduced to him as John Tyler was trying to make a date on the phone. He could hear him clearly without trying to listen. Out of the corner of his eye, he saw another official reading what appeared to be a scurrilous paperback novel. A big sign on the reader's desk announced his name as Rudolph Gonzales, but not what his title was. Two others were walking around in a seemingly aimless fashion, stopping at times to exchange chit-chat with their seated colleagues. He felt the walls closing in. The phone rang. He did not pick it up at once. Was it for him? The man, Tyler, turned and looked at him curiously. Who could be ringing him?

It was his mother. She was trying out the phone, which the Secretariat had insisted on and had installed within hours. He had marvelled at the whole operation. For years he had been trying to get a telephone installed, had filled in form after form, had wasted hours in interviews with evasive officials and had poured out his frustrations in regular letters to the Ministry on the matter. None of this had any effect. First they had told him that too many were waiting to have a phone installed, then that they had no lines and latterly that there were no instruments available. He had given up in disgust.

This swift installation of the phone was another sign that he had done the right thing; the idea that it was a means of checking up on him he refused to consider.

His mother was asking him if he was going to be in for lunch. She told him that Radika had left the house shortly after he had gone and that it was unlikely she would be back soon. The phone, she said, was working excellently. She had already tried it out by ringing up several people. Jagru knew that she wanted to ask if he had heard anything more about his new job. Covering his mouth with his hand so as not to be overheard, he told her that nothing had been settled as yet. He heard her gave a sharp intake of disappointment. She started to tell him that he should try to get settled down quickly so that he would be able to give a helping hand to those in need. He shouldn't forget his original justification for switching parties: that of helping the poor and the needy. Jagru cut her off. He did not want to be too long on the phone with personal matters. He had too many things on his mind.

He wished it was as simple as she imagined. He wondered if he should go and see the man who had interviewed him when he had first made his approach, find out for certain what his new position was. But he knew he could not do that. Men such as his interviewer operated in a different, shadowy field.

He began to walk around like the others. He walked past Mitchell's desk. Mitchell was busy writing on a notepad. He waved to him to take a seat. Jagru sat down.

'What are you doing?' he asked curiously.

'Letters,' Mitchell said, 'to Education.'

'What's going on there?'

'Oh, the usual, I guess.'

Jagru did not pursue the enquiry. He wondered what the 'usual' was.

Mitchell looked up suddenly: 'Got any children?'

'Two.'

'Good schools, eh?'

Only his girl was going to school, Jagru told him. The boy was a baby, not quite three. His daughter, Bharka, had been enrolled into one of the schools near his home. He had not thought of whether it was a good or bad school. It was just convenient. He named the school.

Mitchell pursed his lips. 'Get her into a top school from now, man, then you're not going to have any difficulty later on.'

How did one do that? He had no 'lines'.

Mitchell laughed uproariously. 'That's a good one,' he said when he had finished laughing. 'Where do you think you are? It's time you got reoriented, you know.' He leaned forward confidentially: 'I'm doing this for a friend. He's been trying to get his children into L.O. for a long time; you know, they only take the best. I've talked to the woman and with this letter he'll have no problem. He'll have to go through the usual channels, of course.'

Perhaps it was time to get Bharka into a good school. It would counter Radika's insistence that they send her abroad to her mother. 'Will you write me one of those letters, too?'

Mitchell laughed again, attracting the curious stares of some of the other men. 'You don't need me, man. You don't even need a letter. Just go in and talk to the woman. Tell her who you are and where you coming from.' He gave Jagru a name.

Could he leave, just like that?

'Of course,' Mitchell said, 'I'll tell them you had to step out on some business. Anyway, A.D. don't really check up on us. We're just the reserve, you know.'

Jagru stood indecisively, looking at the paper in his hand. Should he go? It was easy, Mitchell said. Just tell her who he was. But who was he?

He wrestled with this question all the way to the Education Department. The girl at the desk took his name, writing it down laboriously. Did he have an appointment? No? What was his business?

He fumbled. 'Personal.'

The girl raised her eyebrows. 'Personal,' she repeated slowly, as if the word was foreign to her.

'I'm from the Secretariat,' he said.

There was a swift and gratifying change in her manner. Mrs. Smythe would see him in a few minutes. There was someone in with her at the moment.

He sat down and rifled through some outdated magazines. Just a few minutes elapsed when the girl called him again. He made for the door next to her, but he had misread her. What was his position, she wanted to know.

'Liaison Officer,' he told her. That was what he had decided to call himself. It had a good sound to it. How could he tell people that he was an officer II. They would think that he was in some military organisation.

'Hold on,' the girl said and she went into a room.

He stood there, suddenly apprehensive. What was he doing? Was this what he had changed parties to do? He did not wait for the girl to return. He hurried down the stairs. His daughter had a good mind. She would gain top schools for herself. But if there were others who could get in by influence, how many top places would remain? Was there a fair chance that his daughter would get to a good school when she had finished her primary education? He had to work with the system, not fight it. He should go back. What difference did it make if he spoke a few words with someone? It was not as if he was committing a crime. He would not be taking money from anyone or giving it. He wondered how much Mitchell's 'friend' had paid him for the favour. He should go back and explain to the girl that he had suddenly seen someone with whom he needed an urgent word. But maybe it would be better to telephone from the secretariat. Yes, that would be the thing to do. He could ring, explain and apologise and ask for an appointment. His daughter had a right to get a good education.

Mitchell was waiting for him at the Secretariat. 'How did it go?'

'Oh, I had some other things to do. I'm going to ring her and make an appointment for tomorrow.'

'I already rung her and told her you'd be coming. She was expecting you an hour ago.'

As he dialled the Education Department's number, he wondered what Mitchell wanted from him. Why was the man being so helpful? His friendship would surely cost him, if not now, then later.

Someone called his name. There was a messenger at his desk with an envelope to sign for. He felt a dread. It might be his old Party. He hoped they were not going to play tricks on him.

Mitchell hovered over him as he opened the letter. It was from the Education Department. They had sent a form over for him to fill for his daughter's school. He put the form away in his drawer. Mitchell clapped him on the back. Evidently it didn't matter that he did nothing. But why was Mitchell so deliberately making a friend of him? Was the man afraid of something?

After a few days he got used to doing nothing, to being a liaison officer, to behaving as expansively as the rest of the men, although he still chafed inwardly at the waiting.

He made a habit of carrying home his folders and papers and old booklets to peruse, to give the impression that he had a lot of work to do. He made sure he always locked his papers away in his briefcase when he was not looking at them. He started to collect clippings and he already had two which concerned his activities with the new Party. There would be more to come.

He believed what he had told his mother: that they were waiting to make use of him at the right time. He felt sure that it would be so. He began to sweat. He felt that he was sweating a lot these days.

The days moved slowly for Jagru. He was almost surprised to discover how many days had gone by since he had changed parties. Except for the letter from Personnel, nothing. How could they mean for him to go on like this? Eventually he decided to call on Manu and the others, shelving his earlier decision that he should go only when he had real news for them. But they were not at home. They were in the country, visiting one of their many businesses. He regretted not visiting before; he needed someone to talk to.

Asha's casual invitation to her birthday party was constantly in his mind. He hoped she had not been joking. He didn't want to think that she had proffered the invitation simply for the sake of making conversation. He hadn't told Radika yet. She would go to the party carrying as a gift her passive, distrusting thoughts. Why couldn't he put an end to this lukewarm war with his wife? But it was she who had started it, she who in her boredom had begun to pick at him like a nagging middle-aged woman. She had accused him countless times in those early fits of rage. Now he only wished the accusations had been true. He thought of Asha again. Sometimes he tried not to remember her round, rosy face, her lithe body.

At the Secretariat, he saw a lot of women. Not all of them belonged there. He envied the men when he saw them leaving early, their girlfriends draped on their arms. Some of the women at the Secretariat were pretty. Most of them seemed to be kept busy by their extra-curricular activities. From vague scraps of information picked up from their overheard conversations, Jagru had formed definite ideas about their promiscuity. He would keep his distance; they were not his kind of people. Different attitudes and different lifestyles, more free with their affections than he liked his women to be. In any case, what was he thinking of? He didn't want a relationship with any of them. If it was going to be anyone, it would be Asha. But she was always busy, with her many business trips to foreign parts. Would he ever have the courage to make his feelings known to her?

Perhaps, if he thought about it, the work at the Secretariat was beginning to assume some shape. Sometimes, he was asked to tape meetings. He also found himself writing speeches and helping to plan rallies. There were times when he really did liaison work, coordinating events between one Ministry and another. They could not forget him, they would not forget him.

Sometimes, people from off the streets would come in and ask to see him. Some of them he had known when he had been with the old party. They would chat with him a while and then tell him about things that bothered them. He knew there was very little he could do, but often just being able to make their case to him seemed to be enough satisfaction to the people who came.

One day a man came in a rage. What was the Secretariat doing about the cattle rustlers. All his cows were being stolen. He was going to shoot one of the bloody thieving bastards very soon. He was rich, had friends in high places.

Jagru watched as Mitchell blustered. No doubt the man had a genuine complaint. But it was people like him and their money which had helped to put inefficient people into the power structure. Why should he get special treatment when he and others like him had contributed to the general state of affairs. His kind stifled progress, made a fuss about everything and talked loudly about those they knew.

Mitchell was telling the man that he did not take complaints. He must go to the police station. The man was still talking in a loud voice as they ushered him out.

Mitchell shook his head. 'That's not going to do me any good. Putting out a big-shot like that. Somebody's going to get a report on his desk about me. Not that I care anymore.

I've got plans, you know,' he added in a lowered voice.

Jagru nodded, though he had no idea what Mitchell meant. 'They're braggarts, those men,' he said, pointing after the man. 'They make a mockery of the thousands who are really suffering, with their demands to have everything dished out to them on a silver platter.'

Jagru stopped, aghast at himself. These were the sentiments of his old party, directed at the people in the Secretariat and the small group of people who made capital out of knowing them. He looked fearfully at Mitchell, wondering if the man would repeat all that he had said to the wrong person. But Mitchell appeared not to have heard, seemingly caught up in his own thoughts. Jagru went back to his desk. He must be more careful. He had come here to get a position where he could make decisions and favourably influence the lives of the suffering masses. Talking in such a manner was not going to get him anywhere.

One day he visited his daughter's new school. The headmistress appeared overawed as she showed him around the school, flustered and fulsome. She told him how much she had heard of him and how pleased she was to have his daughter at his school. How could she have heard of him? What had he done? It seemed his fame continued to spread before him, despite his inactivity.

Another day his mother surprised him by telling him that she had heard his name mentioned in a food line. He was annoyed; he was earning too much for her to go and stand in lines. Why had she gone back? She told him she was helping out someone who was suffering, someone called Chandi. He had waved her explanations aside, but decided he would make enquiries about the promised food card.

He did not even need a card. He just had to sign his name against the items needed and they would deduct the cost from his paycheck. The items could be collected whenever he was ready. He should have done it before, instead of letting his old mother stand in the lines while he sat around, worrying about his duties and hoped-for appointment.

Mitchell continued to seek his friendship. Did he have a passport, he asked one day.

A passport? Of course, he had one. He had travelled to the nearby countries in the early days, just after he had got his degree.

What about his family?

'Why?' Jagru asked. 'They not planning on going anywhere.'

'You should take them out,' Mitchell advised. 'Prices going up,' he added mysteriously.

Jagru decided it might be best to listen to him. He seemed to be a rich source of information. Yes, it would be wise to take out the passports. He might want to travel when other appointments came along — take his family on holiday, and neither his mother nor his children had passports. Then he found he had a difficulty. His mother would need a new birth certificate. She had lost the original when her bag was snatched one day downtown. He had forgotten about that, but knew how long it could take to get a replacement. One of his former friends at the old party had waited eighteen months.

Eighteen months. Why did all these public departments take so long? Was it all deliberate? Poorly-paid office workers in the Ministries getting their own back? But on whom, those who suffered even more? Perhaps he should forget the passport idea. But why? He should have no problem. He could give someone a call. Mitchell would know who was the right person. He hesitated. Perhaps, he was asking too much of Mitchell. But then, he felt instinctively that when the time came, Mitchell would get his value in returned favours.

The call was made. Before the day was out, the envelope containing the birth certificate was on his desk. Jubilantly, he called across to Mitchell, waving the envelope at him. Mitchell smiled in a forbidding way, his eyes warning him. Again, Jagru regretted his lack of circumspection. Soberly he opened the envelope, then stared in amazement. The certificate was new and crisp and had relevant particulars such as the date and time of birth. Only one thing was wrong with it. A blank space where the name should be. He stared at it for a long, uncomprehending moment, then controlled an impulse to shout for Mitchell. Instead he picked up the phone and dialled again the number which led to the helpful person at the other end.

'Yes, Mr. Bird,' he said, 'yes, I got your envelope. But somebody seems to have made a mistake. My mother's name isn't written on it.… What do you mean there's no mistake? Are you trying to tell me my mother doesn't have a name? Don't be a fool man.' A stupefied look replaced the irritation on Jagru's face as he realised that the man meant what he said. He couldn't figure it out. How could they say that his mother had no name? He put down the phone on the man's apologetic murmurs. Was there something sinister about it or was it just another display of inefficiency on the part of the birth certificate people?

He went across to Mitchell to tell him about the 'no name' birth certificate. As usual Mitchell had a suggestion and told Jagru to leave it to him. The next day, the birth certificate, complete in all particulars, was on his desk and Mitchell was winking at him from across the room. Jagru was learning. After this, getting the passports was no problem, though members of the public were being told that there were no passport books available.

Mitchell had more advice for him. He should host a function soon. Invite all the faces that were known, get people to know him and to feel that they owed him something. It was an excellent idea. He took it up with enthusiasm and was soon on the phone to his mother telling her what he planned. Then he remembered Asha's party and wondered if they were back. He could invite her to his party. Let her see the kind of people he now mixed with. It was clear he had a certain power now, if not an official position. Of course, it was not his intention to misuse such power, but he felt that he had to go along with things, to be seen to be one of them. He had to understand the system first, before he could use it to help others.

The phone on his desk rang. He was both surprised and glad to hear Manu's voice. No static on the line. He had to be calling from nearby. They were back. Manu seemed equally surprised to hear him on the other end of the phone. His voice was cautious. He had meant to ring someone else. Yes, someone in the Secretariat. No, he didn't want Jagru to pass the phone on to the person. No, it was no trouble. He would call back.

Jagru hung up, puzzled. He saw Mitchell's eyes on him. He wondered if he should tell him about the call. He stopped himself. He had to cure himself of this need to discuss every little triviality with Mitchell. After all, there were no real friends in this place.

CHAPTER FOUR

Chandi Panday stood awkwardly at the side of one of the roads leading to the marketplace. She had left the cookshop job. As Aunt Adee had advised, she had got together enough capital to start a little selling business. This had been earned through the work she and her children had done the previous Saturday, hiring themselves out to the foodlines.

'Oranges, oranges,' she shouted. People frequently stopped to buy and some of them even smiled at her. She began to think that the stories of sellers having a hard time were grossly exaggerated. Her complacency was rudely shattered. An ugly-looking man came up to her and kicked her basket aside. Several of the oranges rolled into the road and were immediately squashed by passers-by.

'You tief me spot!' the man hissed.

Chandi tried to protest that she had paid a large sum to the other sellers nearby who had allowed her the spot, but the man, whose hisses progressed to snarls, shouted her down. She gave up and rushed to retrieve her basket which, after several erratic circles, had come to rest in the middle of the road.

But as she was about to do this, a shout went up along the line of vendors.

'The constables coming!'

There was a mad scramble as vendors picked up their goods and ran. They were not allowed to sell on the roads leading to the major markets and were regularly harassed by the market officials. Those who were selling contraband items were at particular risk. Chandi picked up her basket and kept on running until she reached 'Aunt Adee's' stall. It did not actually belong to her, but she was well known around the place and often established squatter's rights for the day. She took Chandi's basket and hid it under the stall.

She told Chandi not to worry, the market constables wouldn't bother her this time, because she had paid her dues. In any event they would soon be scurrying back to their offices inside the market. Not all the vendors were so lucky. One, whose legs had been too slow to escape, had his basket seized, but then the constables, as if satisfied with this perfunctory catch, made an about turn to their offices. Chandi watched as the hapless man followed behind, wringing his hands and pleading. She felt sorry for him, but was glad that it was not she who was running behind them. She could hear him telling the officers that he had many children and large expenses.

The excitement died down. Vendors returned to their spots and began crying out their wares again to passers-by. Chandi told Aunt Adee about the man who had kicked her basket away. He was just one of the big bullies around, Aunt Adee said, she should just ignore him. He would probably not bother her again. Aunt Adee was right. When Chandi went back to her pitch, there was no sign of him. Business became brisk again and soon her oranges were all gone. But she could not leave the market yet. She had told Janki to meet her there so that they could go and buy a new pair of shoes. Her other girls, Artie and Rani, rarely troubled her for new things and often wore each other's clothing, but Janki was the youngest of the girls and often their things could not fit her. Chandi was glad that the profit she had made from the oranges enabled her to afford the new shoes.

The schools had already dismissed for the day. She could see children converging at the bus terminal. What could be keeping Janki?

An hour later, she had become alarmed about her daughter's nonappearance. Perhaps Janki had misunderstood her and had gone directly home. She would have to go and see, but she asked Aunt Adee to keep an eye out just in case Janki turned up.

She was about to leave when she felt a hand on her shoulder. It was a hard, commanding grasp. She turned to look into an unfamiliar face. A man stared at her.

'You Lal Panday's wife?'

Chandi pulled away from his hand. All her fears about her husband's venture into politics resurfaced.

'I don't know what you talking about.'

'I know you, you can't hide.' The man took a step towards her.

Aunt Adee pushed her way in between Chandi and the man. 'Leave she alone, you big bully,' she cried, shaking her fist at him. 'Why you don't go look for you motha!'

To Chandi's relief the man backed off, but then there was a flash in her face. Someone had just taken her photograph. Instinctively she covered her face, but it was too late. She was greatly troubled. Who had taken her picture and why did they want it? It could only have something to do with Lal and his activities and it could not be good. Could this have anything to do with why Janki hadn't come? She hurried home, her fears increasing with each step.

There was no sign of Janki at home. Immediately she dispatched Das to the school to see if maybe she'd been kept in for detention or something, but before she could ask any questions, Artie took her aside and told her that someone had come with a camera and peeped into the shack snapping pictures. She had told the man to leave and threatened to call the police, but he had just laughed in her face and made a nasty suggestion, only leaving when he had finished his business. None of the others had been home at the time and she had decided not to say anything until her mother came home.

Chandi moaned to herself. 'Next time anybody come round here,' she told Artie, 'and you all alone, run across the street and call people. Don't wait to see what happening. We na have any valuables here. He mighta harmed you,' she added, trembling at the thought.

A boy on a bicycle was shouting from the road. He wanted to know if she was Chandini Panday. For a moment, Chandi thought that he might be a school-friend of Janki, but the boy had been sent by Kunti Persaud. Her son was to hold a party soon; there would be some work if she wanted to come.

'Tell Auntie Kunti thanks; I'd be glad to help.' She wondered if she should go at once to Kunti and tell her what was happening, that her daughter was missing and strange men were following her, that her husband was never home during the day and often spent nights away.

Das had returned. 'Nobody at the school,' he told her.

She thought of the many things that could happen to a young, bright schoolgirl and tried not to believe any of them. Her other children were all around her. Nobody knew what to say. They all kept looking at the road, straining their eyes to see if they could make out Janki in the distance. The sun went down. The place was getting dark.

Chandi could no longer pretend that nothing had happened to her daughter; she would have to go the police station.

Then she saw Janki coming around the corner with a

friend. She was laughing. Chandi felt too relieved to even remonstrate with her, but Das shouted angrily, 'Where you think you been all the this time, eh? You think you don't have a home, with nobody to worry about you. Like you drop from tree.'

Janki looked startled. Her friend quickly walked away.

Chandi told Das not to rebuke her. Janki had already begun to pout and Chandi felt that if too many harsh words were said, her daughter might begin to rebel against the shack life. 'We have other things to worry about,' she told Das. 'A man came and took my picture at the market and another one was here. He took pictures of the shack and was very nasty to Artie. I don't think they mean any good. I think we should go and find your father and tell him what is going on.'

But where were the headquarters of the Workers Party? Lal had not even bothered to tell her. 'Do you know where the place is?' she asked Das, who after muttering about having arranged to meet someone, agreed to go with her. He had some idea where the headquarters were.

After a few false starts, they found the place. Her husband was not there, but the woman at the desk, who asked them to call her Mitzi and seemed to know all about Chandi, spoke very kindly. She said that what had happened was harassment and that the Party would know the right forum to take up the matter. She said that the police had no right to harass people because they were political.

Chandi grew more alarmed. She and her children were not political. She could not sit still after that. She made an excuse to leave, telling the woman she had to go and cook.

'You must come back later,' the woman told her, 'when Ban, our leader is here, and don't be afraid. We're dedicated, no matter what the cost, to righting the wrongs of the working class.'

At whose cost, Chandi wondered.

Outside the building, Das was telling her that he had to go meet someone.

'You not going to meet that man again, eh?' she asked anxiously. She couldn't bear to think that Das would be seduced into leaving his books and joining that large, shadowy body of people who were engaged in illegal trade.

'Is just a friend,' Das said, shuffling his feet. 'I still studying you know.'

Chandi watched him go. She would have to work harder; they would have to get a real house soon or else her children would go astray. She was thankful that her youngest, Shyam, had shown no signs of wanting to be with his father, as he had often done before Lal's illness. She was glad for any small mercies that came her way.

★ ★ ★ ★

'It's not enough to say that we can't take it anymore. We must make it plain that we won't take it anymore.' The speaker paused. He was a short man, eyes bulging out of a gaunt face, loose-fitting clothes flapping over his thin body. Lal Panday was alone on the platform, with a microphone which seemed to dwarf him. He should have made a pitiful figure, his defiance ridiculous, but he did not. Indeed, his appearance seemed to lend fire to his words, making his audience listen as if spell-bound. 'Yes,' he shouted, waving his arms as his words rushed at the microphone, 'we must place our lives on the line if necessary. For believe me, my friends, we are already doing this in a place where we must crawl to survive, where we can only live by scavenging for food for our bellies and scuttling into huts at night for shelter. You tell me that you have a job, a roof. Can that job pay your taxes as well as buy the food you need? Can it give your children a good education, too? And tell me, when you've struggled so hard to give your children that education, any kind of education, can they find a good job? How many good jobs are there in this place? Jobs which don't just allow you to exist, but make you proud to be a human being? Who wants their children to be branded as criminals because they too have to take to the streets and the borders to survive, to carry on the so-called illicit trade which is so essential for all of us to get what we need to eat. And they call it criminal. Tell me, my brothers, how much longer must we tolerate a system so divorced from reality, a system which reduces us to a state of animals begging for our own survival?'

'Some may say that I talk because I like to hear my own voice or that I talk of things I do not know. But let me tell you, brothers, that I stand before you as a sugar worker who has toiled in the field all his life and who knows what it is to work hard. I am prepared to work hard. I believe in hard work. My job gave me a shelter over my head. It gave my children bread in their mouths. But the day came when I had to stand back and take stock. I left my job. How could I continue? How could I allow myself to be fed and housed and to be a cog in a system which was allowing so many others to starve? Where was my conscience, my humanity, to support such a system? I stand before you, brothers, an unemployed man. I have no house, no job, no bread. My children live in a shack. Sometimes they get to eat. Sometimes they don't. Do you think that I enjoy the thought that my own wife and children are almost beggars? No, but these are the sacrifices. I have forgotten my own tomorrows and those of my children...'

Lal Panday choked on his words. Out of the silent, mesmerised audience had come a whizzing missile, a piece of glass which struck Lal Panday on the head, abruptly disrupting his speech. He swayed, collided with the microphone and ended up in a tangled heap with it on the floor.

Das had been sitting at the back, drawn by his father's eloquence, but still feeling a deep-seated resentment against the man who had deserted them. He had been sitting there, numbly registering the words his father shouted into the microphone as he wrestled with the problem of trying to understand why his father considered them so unimportant in comparison with his political antics. He had come deliberately, thinking it would be a good place to be while he made his own decision, though part of him had already decided that nothing his father could do or say would have the slightest influence. So what if people were suffering, if there were those who couldn't afford to eat and those who wandered the streets because they had no home. You had to look after your own, didn't you? Didn't charity begin at home? What his father was doing couldn't be anything other than desertion. It was all very well for him to say that the only choice when one left school was to join the smugglers, but his father hadn't done that, had he? No, he had chosen to become a political rat.

At this point in Das's meditations, he realised that his father had been struck down by the missile. In the uproar, he joined the surging crowd trying to get to the platform, but a group of stewards, who had suddenly appeared from a side door, was pushing everyone back. Das stumbled in the crowd.

'It's my father,' he shouted, tears falling down his cheeks. But his words were lost and he was being pushed further away. He flattened himself against a nearby wall in an agony of suspense, just stilling the impulse to throw himself headlong into the crowd, looking for an opening to burrow his way through. What had happened to his father? In that instant Das knew that he loved him and was ready to forgive him all that had happened.

He felt the crowd grow silent. A woman, Ban, the Party leader, had taken up the microphone and was speaking into it. Lal Panday was all right — it had only been a glancing blow — but the meeting was cancelled.

He heard questions. Would they be taking him to hospital and had anyone seen the bastard who had done it? The man was at the microphone again. No, Lal was not going to the hospital. No, he had not really been injured. It had just been a glancing blow.

The crowd slowly dispersed in a babble of voices. Das stood in the shadows, hesitating. His feelings of tenderness toward his father were ebbing, yet he wanted to be sure that nothing was really wrong. He watched for a while. They had given Lal Panday a chair to recover in, but now he was standing up again, having a fierce conversation with someone. Das heard him laugh and resentment and relief flooded him in equal measure. He walked out of the building; his decision had been made. As his father had said, there was only one choice.

★ ★ ★ ★

Manu navigated the dark roadway with a careless ease. He had done this so many times before that charting the many bends and twists in the road had become child's play. Although he did not need to undertake these runs himself, sometimes he did them simply for the thrill of the whole exercise.

Things had gone very smoothly that evening. Indeed, they always did because the right palms were kept well greased. The boat had sailed gently into a little inlet well protected by a bushy shore. He had renewed acquaintances, laughed and whiled the time away, telling the men what was happening in the place of bright lights, as everyone worked quickly, unloading the cargo. Manu had selected what he wanted, paid the price and although he would have liked to have stayed and chatted some more with these men who worked in the dark, it was wise not to hang around any longer than necessary.

He whistled to himself as the car sped along the road, its trunk satisfyingly full. Another hour and he would be home, warm and snug and exchanging gossip with Asha and Bulu and perhaps even scolding the children if they hadn't gone to bed. Only his wife, Delia, would not be there to greet him. He missed her very much, but it had been his decision that she should leave, and when the opportunity had come about a year ago, he had put her on the plane for the richman's country.

She had been full of protests. 'I'm not going Manu, I don't know anyone there. The place is cold-cold. I'll be all alone and think how I'll feel without you.'

'You must go,' he insisted. 'You got to understand. We have to take our chances to leave this place. As soon as the children get their papers cleared, they going to come and join you. And in time I going to come too when I wrap up the business here. You don't think I gon carry on a business like this forever.'

'Who going to look after you, Manu? Who going to look after the children? Who going to iron your shirts, cook the food and see that everything is done properly?'

He had waved away her protests. 'We have to be practical, darling. You know how many people want to leave this place. It's not as if you going to be doing nothing. You gon be going to school, learning things. I going to have a bright wife,' he teased. 'Me, Manu Deo with a bright wife. Who would've thought it?'

Eventually, he had got her around to his thinking, though it had not made the departure at the airport any less painful. As so many times before, this scene came back to him in great detail. He blinked his eyes and found tears dropping on the hand which gripped the steering wheel. He lifted up his other hand, which had been hanging outside the car, to wipe his eyes and in so doing almost missed the sharp glare of the searchlight which greeted him around the next bend.

The car skidded to an abrupt halt. What the hell was some idiot doing flashing the damn thing in his face? And standing on one of the more dangerous bends in the road too. Was he trying to commit suicide? He hadn't thought a policeman's lot was that bad.

He felt for the wad of cash in his pocket. It was not always politic to presume on his friends in high places and to call their names at dark street corners. In any event, he believed in giving the small man his cut of things as well. Everybody had to live. He made his face cheerful as he leaned out of the window.

'Hello, hello, dark night, isn't it,' he said breezily. Beyond the place illuminated by the searchlight, he could make out shadows. The man who had stopped him was not alone. This was going to be a nuisance. He would have to pay more than he expected.

'A good night for some people,' he continued, wondering at the man's silence. Still no response. The others, three of them, had by this time, come up to his car.

He had a wild thought that maybe they were a hold-up gang. He had been a fool to stop. They would take his car and his goods and kill him and leave him by the wayside.

Delia, he thought, am I never going to see you again? All this passed through his mind like a flash, but he could not really believe that his luck would run out on him in this way. It was not written in his fate that he would die like a dog.

The men looked like policemen. He had to believe that they were genuine. He managed a smile.

'What can I do for you, Officers?'

The long pause made him wonder if he could reach the jack handle under the seat next to him without alerting them. But they would have guns, of course. He had been a fool to stop. He should have sped on regardless of the man in the middle of the road. He had been stopped before at roadblocks. Countless times. The men had never been like this. They had always been quick to smile and to exchange greetings and to rub their fingers and thumbs together. And he had always been ready to take the hint and to slip the money in their hands.

After what seemed like a long time, the man who had stopped him said: 'We would like to search your car. We have reason to believe that you may be carrying contraband.'

Manu nodded eagerly. They would find the goods, of course. But he did not care what they found. He knew how to fix it. If they didn't bite, he knew others who would. But of course, there would be no need for that. These men all knew how to line their own pockets. They all wanted a small piece. He felt comfortable again. But as he listened to the sounds of the men examining his car with what seemed to be unnecessary detail, he had the disturbing thought that it might still lead up to a brazen robbery. He gripped the steering wheel tightly. After what seemed like ages, he heard the men close the trunk.

The same man who had spoken to him before was now tapping on the window which he had wound up with great stealth a moment earlier.

'We have to take you in.' There was no apology in the man's voice.'We believe you have things in your trunk which need closer examination.'

Take him? What did they mean take him in? Take him in where? His thoughts were jumping wildly again. It was all just a pretext. They wanted his car, his goods and his money. He sat silent. The man tapped at the glass window again. In a daze, he turned the knob to wind down the glass.

'Fergus going to drive you car. You go with the others,' he said curtly.

Manu got out of the car. It was unreal. Move, move, he urged his paralysed limbs. He waited for the blow on his back or his head. He did not know how he got into the other car, but eventually found himself sitting in the back with one of the men. He watched dully as the man called Fergus drove his car away. The man who had stopped him was still standing by the side of the road, making no move to come into the car. He was whispering to the driver. Manu heard the words 'reinforcements' and 'police station'. Could they really be policemen? Or were they just trying to bluff him, to dull him into a false sense of security? Weren't they supposed to read his rights or something? But was he being arrested or kidnapped? Maybe they were just taking him somewhere to negotiate their price.

At last his car set off and drove for several miles down the dark roads. As it slowed down, Manu saw they were turning into a driveway heading for a building beamed with light. He could just make out the word 'Police' on a faded sign.

So everything was going to be all right after all. He felt like singing. He walked into the station with feverish joy. All his fears had been groundless. How Asha and Bulu would laugh if they knew how jittery he had been.

Inside the station there were not many people. He was given a seat and told to wait until someone could attend to him. He waited for more than an hour without speaking to anyone. Presently, one of the men who had travelled with him in the car brought in a familiar-looking bag. He threw its contents on the counter and began to take an inventory.

Manu smiled indulgently. He sidled up to the man and, in a whisper which could be heard all over the station, said, 'I've got something for you.'

The man did not glance at him. 'We're going to take your statement,' he cautioned. 'Until then, it would be advisable for you not to say anything.'

'But I want to talk to you before *you* say anything.'

The man looked at him now. 'Bribery is a serious offence. I hope that's not what you have in mind.'

Manu was going to say, of course, it was what he had in mind, but he suddenly had the feeling that something strange was going on. He went back to his seat. After a while, another man in officer's uniform came to talk to him. They would have to detain him at the station for the night unless he could raise bail. They had found enough evidence to suggest that he was involved in smuggling.

'Of course,' said Manu, 'of course, I can raise bail.' He was bewildered by what was happening. But until he could talk to some of his friends and find out exactly what was going on, he would have to play ball. He counted out the money from his pocket. A thousand dollars.

The officer counted it in turn, then he said: 'We're going to have to ask for bail in the sum of two thousand.'

Did the man mean he wanted that much as a bribe? That was not part of the game, but then this was a police station where they did not seem to know the rules.

He said eagerly: 'If you'll just let me call someone. I can

get the money in no time.'

The officer's face was grim. 'I'm afraid that's impossible. We can only receive calls during the night. The phones are locked and the officer who has the keys isn't here at the moment. I'm afraid you'll just have to stay here the night.'

Manu looked at the uninviting cell which was situated in a far corner of the station. He gripped the back of his chair. It had a wooden seat, but it had suddenly become comfortable.

'Can I stay here in this chair?' he asked in a more subdued voice.

The officer was indifferent. 'I suppose you can for the time being. You still have to make a statement and I don't know when the man who's handling your case is going to be back.'

Manu hugged the chair, feeling a giddy sense of reprieve. From time to time, he glanced at the looming cell which so far contained only one occupant, a very dishevelled man snoring loudly in what appeared to be a drunken stupor, calling out crazily from time to time. Manu was glad he was not in there. Things could have been worse, but he also thought with a dull anger that they should have never been allowed to get to this stage. He was paying enough people in the right places. He would ring his friend at the Secretariat as soon as they decided that the phone could be unlocked.

He became aware that there was now even less activity around him. The officer who dealt with him had gone and so had the others. A lone man was at the desk; he had just come on duty. Manu smiled at him nervously. To his surprise, he got a smile in return.

'Bad night for some people,' he thought he heard the man murmur.

Manu plucked up his courage. 'A cigarette?'
The cigarette exchanged hands. Silence while he lit it and took a puff. In the cell, the man was still snoring heavily.

'A real bad night,' Manu agreed. 'This has never happened to me before. I don't know what's going on.'

'Special Squad,' the policeman said. 'They started working last night. Picked up quite a few people. Guess they're not doing so well tonight, unless they're doing their grilling elsewhere.'

Special Squad. Manu licked his lip. He should have been warned about this special squad. Yes. He had heard rumblings and talk about the need for scapegoats to whitewash the system. He had not thought about it in relation to himself. He thought that he had oiled the wheels too well for that. But things might still be averted. When they picked him up they had not known about his important connections. He would make the call. Yes, they would soon have him out of here.

He tested the ground. 'Been here five hours now at least. Man, I feel real hungry and would really like to use the phone.'

The policeman was sympathetic. 'Food you're going to get, but the phone...' he shook his head, ''Fraid that's not on until morning. Special Squad policy. They like to give their suspects time for reflection and remorse.. I'm surprised they're not in here grilling you now,' he added. 'They had long, long conversations with the men they arrested last night.'

'This special squad is something new, eh and they keeping it all quiet?' Manu ventured.

'The boys upstairs planning it. They going to rid the country of all this nightrunning and corruption,' the constable volunteered. He shook his head sadly. 'Hard times, hard times. How is a man going to live and feed his children. I don't know.'

Manu asked: 'What's my chance of getting out of here in

the morning?'

'Good, if you can raise the bail. But they're going to put you on trial, you know. Oh, there's going to be a lot of trials.'

Manu could not feel alarm at the thought of a trial, just relief that it was not part of their plan to keep him indefinitely locked up. He knew that such things had been done, when the authorities decided that it was not in the public interest for suspected persons to walk freely. Suspected person. The words had a hateful sound. But he would not long be that. As soon as he walked out of the station in the morning, he would put things right. He had been putting things right for a long time. Coffee was being offered. It smelt fresh. Manu took a greedy sip. It was good coffee, not the kind that was processed in the country. Someone like him must have brought in such coffee. How could the mighty condemn him and men like him when their own system failed? They were just cutting off their noses to spite their faces. This new policy would not last. His kind was needed. But the idiocy was that a few scapegoats would have to pay to help polish up their tarnished image. He was determined that it wasn't going to be him languishing in any prison cell. As soon as he was released, he would see how things were going and make the right move.

Delia. He thought of her longingly. So long since he had seen her. The policeman was talking to him again, asking a friendly question. He turned his thoughts to the conversation which was opening up. The night did not seem so weary now. Soon, it would be morning.

CHAPTER FIVE

A bomb. In the Secretariat.

Feet reacted faster than the speed of the news as people hurtled through doors to distance themselves from the possible explosion. Within minutes, it seemed everyone was outside. Sirens sounded and the PM's car was glimpsed in ignominious flight. Other executive cars followed.

Several hundred, Jagru among them, stood at what was deemed a safe distance, waiting.

'Wonder what he was doing here, the PM? Nearly got caught in that madness,' Mitchell hissed at him.

An assassination attempt? Jagru didn't voice the thought.

'Perhaps there isn't any bomb,' he volunteered as time dragged by. Someone picked up his words and speculation soon became certainty that it was just a scare.

A bomb squad eventually arrived.

'Back off,' one of the men shouted at the waiting crowd as they went into the building. A couple of hours later, they came out still grim-faced. No bomb.

Jagru found himself among the organisers shepherding the workers back into the Secretariat. The excitement, and in some cases secret hope, was over, but the scare brought changes. From then on, platoons of guards were littered all over the place. Two had been placed at the door leading to Jagru's department and although they knew Jagru very well, they punctiliously demanded his identity card each time he entered the Secretariat. Jagru wondered how long it would be before they started to search people and to check their briefcases. He knew instinctively that if they ever instituted that kind of search on any member of the staff, it would be a signal to that person to get the hell out of there. He was still busy doing very little as far as official work was concerned although a few days ago his hopes had been raised that something was going to happen. Nothing had. He tried not to dwell on the half-formed conclusion that they were playing with him, laughing at his anxieties and hopes. Now he was trying to keep busy planning his goodwill party, compiling a masterlist with Mitchell's help. When he was not planning the party, his thoughts dwelt on Asha. He had even admitted to himself that he was probably in love with her, that he was glad that relations between himself and his wife were at their lowest ebb.

He had begun to feel a little more hopeful after the incident of the bomb scare. He sensed a difference in the atmosphere. Other staff members, whom he had only known by sight, began to talk to him. One of the men, Carl Blair, who sat in a plush office beyond his department and had an executive title, condescended not only to notice him, but had given him instructions and temporarily put him in charge of what amounted to a post in his section. This had been his first evidence that their department had some link to the other offices, had some direct connection. He had begun to think that they were on a desert island, each man on his own. What particularly pleased Jagru was the way Blair had gone about praising him afterwards. But he couldn't understand *why* the man had showered such praises on him for simply helping to organise things after the bomb scare. He had certainly not acted beyond the call of his duty as Blair's words seemed to indicate.

'Mr Persaud,' Blair had said, 'is a fine example of the kind of person we need at the top. Rest assured that we will make good use of you. Your prompt actions will not be forgotten.' Blair had gone on in this way for several minutes at a hastily-called meeting whose members came mainly from Jagru's department.

He had gone on to speak about the need to ferret out moles, spoke darkly of sabotage and hinted that some strategy was being formulated to strike a decisive blow for political recovery.

If Jagru had still been with his old party, he would have thought 'aha', at last they are making admissions that things are not as bright as they liked to maintain, but he was still trying to absorb what appeared to be unmerited words of praise about himself and only passively registered the rest of the speech. There had to be some point to Blair's fulsome words.

But a day passed, two days passed. Nothing. He would have been forced to resume his preoccupation with such trivialities as planning his party had he not suddenly become aware of the growing tension in his department.

Someone was walking around whom he had never seen before and no one bothered to introduce. He slouched around in a sinister way and seemed to enjoy rifling through the contents of people's desks.

Jagru watched him with a scowl. Mitchell shook his head slightly in warning. To hell with it, Jagru thought. He didn't understand what was going on and he didn't care. He would ring Asha, see if she was still going to hold that birthday party of hers and maybe if he could scrape up his courage, ask her to go to lunch with him. His hand moved toward the phone. But it rang before he could pick up the receiver.

It was Manu. Jagru started to exchange pleasantries with him when he was abruptly cut off. A wrong number. He had not meant to ring Jagru. He had another urgent call to make. They would talk some other time. Jagru was puzzled. He wondered who Manu was trying to call at the Secretariat and why the call was always being routed to his desk. He didn't have to be a genius to realise that it was all connected with Manu's business, but if Manu had a friend in this office, he felt better not knowing anything about it. He remembered the words Blair had used about cleaning things up.

He felt eyes boring into his back. He turned around to surprise a look of intense, almost agonised concentration on the face of John Tyler, one of the men in the place who didn't talk much with anyone, but seemed to spend a lot of time on the phone. Jagru wondered. He caught Mitchell's eye on him. He was waving a piece of paper. Why was Mitchell trying to pass him notes? What was wrong with speaking?

He got up and walked in what he felt was a careless manner past Mitchell's desk. The piece of paper was slipped with much stealth into his hand. He read the note and almost laughed. It was an invitation to the canteen. What was Mitchell playing at? But there was no answering laugh from Mitchell. He looked grim.

They met in the canteen. Mitchell whispered, 'How do you like being under investigation?'

Jagru almost jumped out of his skin.

'What investigation?' The words came out too loudly and curious gazes were turned in their direction.

Mitchell hushed him. 'I mean the department, all the offices, the whole Secretariat. They're starting from the very top, you know. Didn't you hear Blair say there was going to be a clean up? More than a few heads will go on the chopping block.'

Jagru was silent, bitter. Was he in the wrong place at the wrong time? 'I haven't done anything,' he managed at last.

'You don't think they always pick the guilty, do you?' Mitchell said softly. 'But I don't expect you've anything to worry about,' he laughed shortly. 'You're still too valuable. Just thought I'd give you a friendly warning. So you wouldn't give too many howls of protest if the Mr Browns of this world come wandering around the office, picking at your possessions and asking you nasty questions.'

Jagru had the clear impression that once again Mitchell had something to hide. If this whole clean-up business was a fair and sincere effort to put a better system in place, Jagru thought he would welcome it. Wasn't that what his long dedication to the struggle was all about, why he had walked out on his old colleagues?

Mitchell muttered something about getting back to his desk. Jagru sipped his coffee slowly, ignoring the now familiar watery taste.

The man he had seen earlier in the office was coming through the door. He raised his hand to Jagru, then came over to his table. 'Ah, Mr. Persaud,' he said in an overloud voice, 'I saw you earlier, but you were preoccupied, so I didn't want to disturb you. I'm told you're the very man to help.'

'I'm sorry,' said Jagru, 'I don't think we've met.'

The man laughed: 'I'm Brown. Gordon Brown. In charge of the corruption investigation.'

Jagru drank the last of his coffee. 'Sorry. Just remembered something important I've got to do.' He got up quickly and hurried back to his desk, not fully understanding his aversion.

★ ★ ★ ★

Asha got slowly out of bed. It was late and she could hear the jangling sounds of vehicles going by in the street below and snatches of conversations from passers-by. She pulled the blinds back quickly and immediately regretted her action. She had been busy last night, delivering goods to some of the retailers they supplied and had gone to bed late. The sharp sunlight which streamed in from the windows made her blink and scattered some of her drowsiness. She unbuttoned her nightgown and let it fall to the floor. Naked, she walked languorously towards the bathroom.

The cold water cascaded down her long, black hair, making it cling to her body. She soaped herself vigorously and traced the soapy water down her legs, beginning to feel alive. In a few days, she would be twenty-seven. It was a glorious age to be, but it was time she started doing something more with her life than just gadding about the place, dashing in and out of airports to facilitate their business. Once she had felt that what she was doing amounted to a real service for the thousands who depended on what they called 'the people's trade' to feed themselves and their children. Now she was beginning to tire of it all. The excitement was fading; the anger at the system which fuelled her need to outwit it had dulled considerably. She was beginning not to care. Constant exposure to countless examples of suffering was beginning to make her immune. It was time for a change, a time to seek different horizons. She wasn't going to indulge in a head-on battle with their rulers — those who tried were fools who always failed — though perhaps they had their place in the scheme of things. She was tired of it all. It was time to decide.

She was sure that the future was somewhere else — where life was not just a constant battle of wits in a world gone mad. She felt she had often been too busy to think seriously, and then again, you got used to the idea of just existing without considering the pros and cons of it all. Perhaps all this thinking was just the approach of her birthday. Twenty-seven years! It seemed a lot. Asha laughed away the thought. She was young. She would always be young. Gloriously young.

The telephone began to ring, insistently. She towelled herself unhurriedly. Manu's two boys would already have left for school, but Bulu was probably somewhere in the house. She listened for the sound of footsteps moving toward the phone. Nothing. Blast! Perhaps she was the only one in. She wrapped the towel around her and opened the bathroom door. The phone had stopped ringing. She shrugged and continued drying her hair. Manu would probably be home soon. Why did he still make trips like that? There was really no need. The goods would have been delivered anyway. Perhaps it was because he missed his wife. He was a good man, Manu. He would never dream of looking at another woman. He, Bula and herself had all been thoroughly grounded in the rights and wrongs of things — and then he was really fond of Delia. They all got along so well together. Perhaps she would join Delia soon. Even get enrolled at the college where Delia was studying. She had always wanted to study further. Had the time come to leave?

The phone was ringing again. This time, Asha managed to reach it in time. At first she did not recognise the voice.

It was Jagru, but he sounded different, almost breathless, as if he had been running. She teased him, asking him if his new post was so hectic. Had they made him a minister yet?

Jagru mumbled that nothing had been said as yet about a ministerial post. Then his voice became cool and collected. Asha suspected that he wanted the post very badly. She moved to lighter topics.

'I saw Radika a number of times in town yesterday,' she laughed. 'We seemed to be bumping into each other quite a lot, as if we were following each other around.' She heard Jagru mumble something about his wife liking to go shopping. Then at last he got around to the point of his call, that he was planning a party for some new friends and he wanted her to come. It was to be held shortly after her birthday.

Asha started. 'I'd forgotten about holding a party. I've been so busy lately... I think we'll just hold a small dinner instead. You're invited, of course, and Radika.'

'Oh thanks.' Awkward pause.

'Anything else?'

Jagru rushed into speech.

'I wondered if I might — I mean if I might drop by later — in the evening, that is?'

'Of course. You generally do anyway.'

'Yes, yes. But since you've all been away —'

'Well I probably won't be in. But Manu and Bulu —'

'I was hoping to see you, actually.'

'Oh.'

'Perhaps we could meet. I mean over a pre-birthday lunch, you know. Discuss something, I mean advise me on something.'

'Well I don't really know. Not sure about what I'll be doing.'

'I'd really like to see you.'

'Can I get back to you?'

'Of course,' Jagru breathed out slowly. 'Could you let me know tomorrow? Listen, did Manu get through?'

'What do you mean?'

'Well, he called here earlier. He's always getting my desk by mistake.'

'Oh, I really don't know. Just got up actually. None of

them seems to be in.'

'Got to go now,' Jagru lowered his voice, conscious of Tyler's eyes boring into his back. 'Can't monopolise the phone for personal matters.'

'Nice chatting to you,' Asha said.

'I hope, I hope to see you tomorrow.' Jagru tried not to make his voice too eager.

What personal matters? She bade him goodbye.

But what was Manu up to? Where was he?

The phone rang again. It was, at last, him.

'Where are you?' she asked.

Manu was still at the Police station where he had spent a sleepless night and a frustrating morning. The friendly policeman had left, though another who also seemed inclined to be friendly had taken his place. Manu felt that if it had been up these two, he would have spent his night between comfortable sheets, instead of on the hard bench.

He had not seen the men who picked him up. He was told that they would be around later. He was given a very scanty breakfast and had been allowed to use the phone. He thought at first that he would call his friend at the Secretariat. He had reached Jagru instead. Jagru was friendly, of course, but he had never really sounded him out on their business and might be mistaken about his views. He didn't want Jagru to know whom he was calling, and said he would call back. On reflection, he thought it wiser not to do so. The matter was too delicate for the telephone. He tried his home.

He heard Asha's horrified gasp as he explained what had happened and how he was still at the police station. She promised to leave immediately with the money. He had to spell the name of the place and give her directions. He felt cheered. When he was back home they would hold a family conference. Perhaps, it would be wise not to do any more business for a while until the Special Squad had satisfied their zeal.

* * * *

At lunch time, Jagru decided to forgo the usual snack at the canteen and go for a walk. It was far too hot, but a cool breeze swept by, fanning his perspiring body. A car honked beside him. Mitchell with the offer of a lift.

'Best to avoid the Old Square today,' he advised mysteriously.

'Just going to the High Street,' Jagru muttered.

Mitchell was off for the afternoon, visiting friends. He didn't elaborate and Jagru avoided the unspoken invitation to exchange confidences. Jagru wasn't meeting anyone. A bit aimless. But perhaps not so, if it removed him from the Secretariat's gloom for a few hours.

Walking past the shops, thinking about Asha and hoping he would see her the next day, he bumped into a group of schoolgirls who giggled and gave him bold stares. Jagru averted his eyes, feeling awkward.

At the end of the High Street, he found himself making his way to the Old Square.

Damn Mitchell. Why did he always listen to the man like a lap dog? Some people were staging a protest march in the Square. A woman was leading the marchers. About eleven men. As Jagru watched, he found himself in the grip of a tightening in the pit of his stomach which claimed kinship with the group and it was all he could do not to cross over and join them. He pressed panic buttons. What was he doing here? Was it safe? With an effort, he turned and walked away.

★ ★ ★ ★

A police van pulled up. Several plainclothes men trundled out. Ban, the leader of the group, protested as they began to bundle the marchers into the van.

'We have permission for this march,' Ban said.

'Oh yeah, you and who else?'

'Look, here it is.' Ban held out a piece of paper.

'This isn't signed by the Police Chief.'

'Well, here we go again,' said Ban. 'Another rigmarole.'

'Just get in the frigging van, lady.'

'Keep your hands to yourself, sleazebag. I don't need your kind of help. Oh hello, Lal.'

A panting Lal Panday came up to the van and was roughly pushed aside by one of the men. 'I'll get a lawyer,' he shouted.

'Just routine. You'll get used to it. Out on bail or something soon.' Ban's voice was cheerful despite the menace shown by the men arresting her.

An hour later, they were set free, after their very voluble lawyer had turned up demanding that they be charged or released.

'You can go,' said the man who had arrested them, seeming suddenly to tire of the game.

'See you around in court or somewhere else.' Ban gave a mock salute as she left.

★ ★ ★ ★

The three school girls walked into the department store, holding hands and giggling between the words they whispered to each other. They seemed absorbed in their conversation and as they walked through the store, their hands strayed in a careless fashion to touch the various items as they passed. They tried to appear self-possessed, their fleeting homage to the clothing and fineries they touched intended as an imitation of the way they believed sophisticated shoppers behaved. When they felt confident that their chatter and laughter, with the general noise around them, were sufficient cover for their activities, they picked up small items and cleverly hid them in their bosoms and in their books. Janki Panday tripped along with them, a little nervously, but just as eager to lift things as her friends, Pansy and Lily.

The day before, they had 'done' another store and had got away with so many things that much of Janki's fears had been dispelled. She had ceased to worry what would happen if they were caught, about what her mother would say if she knew. It was so exciting to have ribbons and new slides for her hair, stockings and even a new belt, as well as a pair of earrings. All these she had picked up yesterday. She had not taken them home, for there was no place to hide them, but had left them with her best friend, Lily, who had a secret hiding place in the room which she had all to herself. Lily came from a rich home and had lots of friends. But she had chosen Janki to be her best friend. Janki was pleased and very conscious that she could not hope to be like Lily in the way she attracted friends and the way she dared to do things. But she could try. And when Lily had still wanted her friendship even though she knew they had been thrown out of their house, Janki felt that she could not do enough to show Lily what this meant to her.

They had gone downtown and had so much fun. Yes, it had been real fun and they had all those nice new things to show for it. They would do it again and again. This time Janki had agreed more willingly. She had already stuffed her bosom with a scarf which she found irresistible.

Lily turned to her: 'Janki, I must have that blouse.'

Janki looked at the blouse. It was beautiful. She giggled: 'Have it then.'

'Can't,' Lily giggled back. 'Already have too much stuff,' she patted her bosom which seemed to have expanded alarmingly in the past half hour.

'Ask Pansy,' Janki suggested.

'Can't,' Lily said. 'She got too many things too.'

Janki giggled. She could do it, she thought. The scarf had taken up much room, but she could push the blouse further down. 'I'm going to look fat,' she said.

'Here's your chance,' Lily whispered. 'Grab it fast.'

Janki grabbed. At the same time, a hand came down on her back. The others were also grabbed in the same unceremonious manner. The guard at the store had been watching the girls almost as soon as they entered. He knew the ways of school girls, had caught several of them before, picking up things to hide in their clothing. He marched the three girls to the office.

Janki trembled. She thought of her mother and how sad and worried she would be. She felt like sinking through the floor. Pansy had started to cry. But Lily was not crying. Lily was shouting, telling the store people that her father was a very important man and he would make them all lose their jobs.

'My daddy is going to fix all of you,' she raged. 'Just you wait. Wait until I tell him how you grabbed me on the back. Assault and battery and rape,' she added for good measure.

The store people were not impressed. A woman manager said: 'You can tell it all to the police, my girl.'

Lily put on a further show of bravado. 'Bah,' she said, 'my father is bigger than any police.'

Janki was trying to clutch Lily's arm. She could see that

the store people were becoming angry at the way Lily was 'flying' her mouth. It was all right for Lily to talk. Lily's family would see that no harm came to her. Poor Pansy was still crying in a corner. As for Janki, her body had began to shake violently. She had a terrified image of the girl's school to which, it was said, bad girls were sent. Most of all she dreaded the thought of her mother learning about it all. She had so many problems and Janki felt ashamed to be adding to them. She started to cry.

Lily had stopped talking. The store people left them in a little room, saying that they would be back shortly.

Pansy said: 'Lily, what's going to happen?'

Lily shook her curls defiantly. 'They'll have to let us go. My father will see to it.'

'Suppose he doesn't find out, suppose they don't let us call anybody, but just keep us locked up,' Pansy wailed.

Lily was scornful: 'We've got our rights. They can't keep us here for long. They're just trying to frighten us, you'll see. They'll have to let us go.'

'They caught us red-handed,' Janki said. 'We were stealing. They'll say we're thieves. They'll lock us up. We'll never see our families again.'

Pansy began a fresh burst of crying. Lily said impatiently: 'Don't let them frighten you. If we think like that they'll think they can do anything with us... They took our names and addresses. I'm sure they're going to call our dads. My father won't let them give us to the police. Don't worry.'

Call their dads, Janki thought. But how could they? Her parents had no phone and it was possible that nobody would be home at this time. She didn't really want her mother to know what she had done, but it was better than bringing the police in. Her mother would cry and be upset and she would feel awful for days. But she would be home and safe and sound. She even felt good about the thought of being home in the shack. But how could they come for her? They wouldn't know what had happened and Ma wouldn't come. Lily's father would come for her and so would Pansy's. She would be left all alone. She continued to sniff, wishing she had never listened to Lily.

The door opened and a man came in. The guard and the woman manager were with him. 'I'm a policeman,' he told the girls. 'We're trying to contact your parents. We might have to charge you, but if your parents come, you'll be released into their custody.'

Both Lily and Pansy brightened at this, but Janki felt more depressed. She had given the address of the shack. No-one would be home.

The store manager said: 'Of course they must be charged. I want to make an example. These school girls are a real nuisance. They're always coming into the store stealing things. They must have cost me a fortune already. I don't care who their fathers might be. I'm not going to let this matter drop.'

Pansy ran to hold onto her hands: 'Please, please, Miss Lady,' she begged, 'please let us go. My mother will pay you for the things I took. I promise you we'll never do it again.'

'I'll never do it again,' Janki added. 'I'll never do it again.'

'It was just a joke. We didn't mean anything. My father will pay. He'll pay for everything,' Lily said. She had finished with her tantrums.

The manager's eyes glittered: 'He'll pay, will he. We'll see about that.'

'I had my eye on them as soon as they entered,' the guard was telling the policeman. He stopped when there was a knock on the door and a man in an expensive-looking grey suit entered. Lily ran to throw her arms around him.

'Daddy,' she squealed, 'Daddy, I'm terribly sorry, I'll never do it again.'

Lily's father extricated himself. 'We'll have to have a little talk about this. I think I'm going to have to take you away from all this temptation, eh,' he said. He looked at Janki and Pansy: 'So these are your other partners in crime?'

'Daddy,' Lily said, her face all smiles, 'I promised them you'd be able to take care of everything. I told them everything would be all right when my daddy came.'

'You did, eh. Well, we'll have to see about that.' He turned his attention to the adults in the room. 'So what is the situation. If I pay for what the girls took, will you drop the matter?'

There was a hurried consultation. The policeman said: 'It's not going to be as easy as that, Sir, the owner wants to press charges.'

'But surely, you can see they're just children, man. They're genuinely sorry for what's happened and I'm sure it will never happen again.'

The manager said: 'I want to make an example of them. They may not do it again, but others will.'

'I'm sure we can settle the matter without too much fuss,' Lily's father replied. He went closer to speak to the policeman and the store lady. The girls could not overhear the conversation. After a while, they heard the manager say: 'Well, I guess your daughter can go in your custody. But she's been very rude to me. She must apologise first. And I'm not sure at this stage that I'm going to drop the charges.'

Lily turned a jubilant face to the others. 'We're going to get you out,' she whispered reassuringly. She muttered an apology to the woman. Then she was out of the door, chattering away to her father as if the incident had never occurred.

Half an hour later, Pansy's mother arrived and, after a tearful scene and a lot of recriminations on her part, they too left.

Janki was alone.

The policeman spoke to her in a kindly voice. He told her that they had been unable to contact her parents, that the manager was not willing to let her go, suspecting she had given them a false address. He might have to take her along to the station where she would be held. Meanwhile, they would contact her school and try to reach her parents again.

Janki's heart sank in dread.

★ ★ ★ ★

'Now Shyam, a brave boy like you na must cry,' said Aunt Adee, raising her voice above the din of the marketplace, as she awkwardly patted the little boy on his shoulder.

'The man,' sobbed Shyam, his shoulders heaving as he jerked the words out, 'the man act like I was begging. He gave me 25 cents, he gave me...' he began a fresh wave of crying.

'Well,' Aunt Adee said, 'did you ma na explain that you helping out? You a strong little boy, too. You going to grow stronger, you know and one day, you going to be a big boy able to do many things.'

Shyam brightened at this. 'Will I get very strong, Aunt Adee? Will I be able to carry heavy things and do all the work for Ma.'

'Of course, you going to be very strong. Stronger than any of the ragamuffins about this place,' Aunt Adee said as she gave him a lollipop.

Shyam sucked contentedly. He flexed his arm. 'Look, Aunt Adee, I going to grow very strong and I going to beat anyone who calls me a beggar.'

But Aunt Adee was not listening to him. 'Look, here is your mother! Lord, what new trouble is this?'

Chandi was looking most agitated. She dragged a half-filled basket of oranges behind her, while Artie carried a smaller basket in her arms.

'Aunt Adee!' Chandi was shouting even before she had arrived near the market stall. 'Aunt Adee, they hold up Janki. I got to go to court. I got to see what's happening to my poor baby. Keep these baskets until I come back. Shyam, you stay here with Aunt Adee and guard these baskets. Be a good boy now.'

'What she do?' Aunt Adee asked.

'They say she thieve from the store,' Chandi said, wringing her hands. 'I got to go.' She rushed off with Artie following closely behind.

'Aunt Adee, they going to lock up Janki?' Shyam asked.

Aunt Adee didn't answer immediately. She stared after the receding figures of Chandi and her daughter. 'Poor woman,' she muttered. 'Poor woman.'

'They tell me court seven, they said this is where they try all children cases.' Chandi, her face bewildered, clutched at the woman who was dressed in a constable's uniform and whom she had accosted in the courts' corridor.

'They do hold most of the children's cases in court seven,' Constable Smith confirmed, 'but some are held in court six as well. What case you have?'

'My daughter, Janki,' Chandi said wildly. 'I selling at the market and I get a message that they pick her up stealing in the stores and that they have her at the court and that I must come quick. I been checking all the courts back and forth, but nobody knows anything about it. My poor daughter, I don't know what they done to her. Please help me find her.'

Constable Smith thought for a moment. She was in a hurry, but she could spend a few moments trying to help out this woman in her distress. She noted the slight bulging of the woman's waistline and remembered how even trivial things had magnified and upset her when she was carrying her own son. 'If you give me some details, I might be able to help. You know the name of the store your daughter was picked up in, or the name of the officer handling the case?'

'I know nothing. Nothing. All I know is that they arrested her, and sent a message that I was to go to court. My poor child!'

'Well, I don't know what I can do to help you. You could try waiting at the bottom of the court. They may be bringing the case to court later. They have to prepare statements, you know. It's very rarely done all in one day.'

'You mean they going to hold my Janki in some lock-up until they decide they ready to go to court?'

Constable Smith shrugged. 'Of course, they may not be bringing any case to court. They may have just given her a warning.'

Sharp pains lanced through Chandi's stomach. She felt sick with imagining what might be happening to Janki while she could do nothing. She grasped at this straw of hope.

'You really think they might have let her go...? But why I was told to come to court?'

'Why not go to the Central Station down the road here,' Constable Smith said. 'They might be able to tell you more. Who knows, you might have got a wrong message... I'm sorry, but I've got to go now,' she added gently. She walked away, knowing that if she didn't hurry, she would be late for the afternoon session where she performed as a court orderly. She felt pity for the woman. Too many children were being dragged before the courts these days. She hated it. It wasn't always their fault. It was the break-up of family life. She loathed seeing children in court, their sad, lost expressions as they listened to the charges against them clothed in grand-sounding words. Indeed, more and more, she was coming to hate the whole procedure of people being dragged before the courts.

She knew she should feel differently. Law and order were necessary; lawbreakers, especially those with real criminal intent, had to understand that they couldn't break the law with impunity. Perhaps it was because she was in one of the small courts, where the offences people were being charged with often seemed so ludicrous, that she felt so depressed. There were those who came before the courts for selling goods where they shouldn't be selling and selling what they shouldn't. There were raggedy pickpockets, often young children, and the political people picked up for marching without permission or for creating a public disturbance.

People often came to ask for her help, to find out about their court files and sometimes to intercede with the clerks on their behalf in such matters as paying bail. She wasn't always able to help. She was only an orderly, making sure there was order in the courtroom, calling out names, passing documents between the magistrate and the lawyers.

Sometimes, that political woman would come, the one who didn't care how she dressed, with the huge note book in her hand to take down everything that happened in the courtroom. She didn't know her real name. She called herself Ban. Quite why she came she wasn't sure, except that it was meant to irritate the authorities, and certainly, the magistrate was always irritated whenever he saw Ban in court and always looked to her as if he expected her to eject the woman summarily. But he never said anything, although his eyes never strayed from Ban's busy pen, the moment she sat down at the table reserved for the press, feverishly taking down everything that was said. Ban's party produced an occasional newsletter and so the magistrate did not dare to order that she be removed from the press section.

She occasionally exchanged words with Ban who had told her once:

'Some of them making a mockery of justice. But when they see me and my friends, sitting there faithfully recording everything that goes on, they got to be careful. After all there're higher courts and in the end, a higher court to answer to. We're going to record everything that goes on and when the time comes we'll show their justice for the mockery it is.' Ban had complained that there was a a particular magistrate who just counted convictions on his belt and thrived on the publicity.

She had inwardly sympathised, but, of course, she couldn't say so, or indeed be seen talking too often to Ban. She felt the magistrates were not too pleased about it. She had heard strange stories about Ban, too. It was well known she had once supported the Official Party and had been very active in it before she suddenly left to form her own. People said that she had become disillusioned with some of the things she had witnessed, and that when they had put her in jail for challenging the leadership, she had beaten drums at night and held conversations with the spirit world. But these might just be stories. Perhaps it was best not to pay too much attention to them. Would Ban go over to record cases in the new court which was being formed? This was the 'Additional Court', so called, where the 'office crimes' would be heard. It seemed that a whole wave of people were being charged with embezzling and corruption and things like that. She had heard that she might soon be assigned to the

Additional Court. It would at least be a change from the shufflings of this one she thought, as she entered the courtroom, though she also wondered whether, but for the grace of God, she too might have become one of those standing trial for stealing from their remote state employers. She was glad that she had never been placed in a position of financial trust or given an opportunity to steal. She might easily have done it, for God knew her pay was meagre enough. She gave thanks for her friend Robin who helped her out and made the small pay less important. Robin was in the 'Trade', and often she toyed with the idea of quitting her job and joining him. However, it was her very experience of the courts, seeing so many brought there for being in the trade, that made her feel the risk was too great.

She took up her position in the court room. The magistrate had arrived in his chambers and would soon be starting the proceedings. She saw a girl, sitting on the first bench reserved for defendants. Could she be the girl the woman was seeking? But as the girl turned, she saw that she was much older than the woman's description of her daughter.

Then she became aware that the magistrate was in his doorway, trying to attract her attention.

'All rise,' she bellowed, but as she carried out her duties of shouting the defendants' names as the magistrate picked up their files, she still wondered how the woman was faring in her search for her daughter.

Chandi was not faring well.

'You stay here,' she told Artie, pointing to a spot near the stairs, leading to the courts. They might bring Janki while she was away looking for her at the station and it would be unbearable if nobody was there to support her. She told Artie that if Janki did turn up, to send a message quickly with someone, even if she had to pay to deliver the message.

Artie nodded, tears in her eyes. She had been at home when Janki's friend, Lily, came to tell her what had happened. In great agitation she had run all the way to the market to tell her mother. Now she felt like crying as she watched her mother hurry out of the gates of the court building and then turn back. She leaned forward eagerly. Had her mother seen Janki coming? No, it was only to give her some money, in case she needed to pay for anything.

Chandi was just leaving again when a shabbily dressed man, who was standing nearby, clutched at the sleeves of her dress.

'You don't need bail money,' he whined. 'I carry you to someone who'll lend you their property deeds for a few hours so you can pledge it as security for bail. It won't cost you much. Just a small fee for the loan. We help no matter how big the bail. What's your daughter going to jail for?'

Chandi shook off his hand. She didn't quite understand what he was saying, but the word 'jail' had inflamed her. 'My daughter isn't going to jail, you old wretch,' she shouted. 'Get out of my sight!'

'You going to be sorry,' the man muttered and moved off.

Chandi felt out of breath. The effort had taxed her and she felt the now familiar pain in her belly. She pressed her hand to it and began to walk quickly down the road, towards the police station.

There, nobody knew what she was talking about. They sent her to the department which they said was in charge of prosecutions. The people there knew nothing about it. She was becoming more frantic. What had they done with her daughter? Someone suggested that Janki might still be at the store.

'Which store?' she demanded.

No one could answer her. She was going round in circles, moving from section to section to see if she could glean anything, any scrap of information about her daughter's whereabouts. It was useless. The girl was just not there. They had no knowledge of any shoplifting report involving her. In the end they had to forcibly remove Chandi because of the uproar she was making.

She walked back to the courts in a trance-like state, her body racked by pain. Time was passing so fast. What if they closed the courts and she did not find Janki? She would take Artie and go check all the big stores. Maybe Artie might be able to find the girl who had brought the message.

From a distance, she could make out Artie, standing talking to two others. Surely that was Rani and who was the other? She strained her eyes. No, it couldn't be. But it was. It was Janki. She broke into a run, ignoring the heaviness of her body and almost tripping in her haste.

She threw her arms around her youngest daughter. 'Janki, Janki,' she was laughing and crying, 'I get so worried. I think all kinds of things happen to you.'

Janki, filled with remorse, hugged her mother. She would never forget the lesson of the day. She would never again touch anything that did not belong to her. They had kept her for hours in that store, waiting for someone from her home to arrive. As the hours passed and no-one did, she thought that maybe Lily had forgotten to take the message. She refused to believe that they might have got the message and not come for her.

Eventually, a teacher from her school had arrived. It was Miss Dilly. Janki never really got on well with her. She was always scolding her and making her look a fool in front of the class. Recently, Miss Dilly had taken to calling her 'your highness'. Somehow she must have found out where she now lived and was mocking her. Otherwise Janki could never understand why Miss Dilly picked on her.

When Miss Dilly arrived at the store, she had arched her eyebrows and smiled in a nasty sort of way. 'So pilfering, eh, and caught at it, too. Tut, tut,' she had murmured, before engaging in a long whispered conversation with the policeman. The result was that they had allowed her to leave with Miss Dilly, but only after the teacher had undertaken to see that she turned up at the station the next day in case there were any charges.

Miss Dilly, who had simpered and smiled at the policeman and the other people in the store, kept quiet until they were out of earshot, then she had blasted Janki's ears with a tongue-lashing about young tarts who gave their school a bad name. Filled with shame and remorse, Janki had kept quiet.

When she turned up at the court with Rani in search of her mother and heard how harassed she had been, she wished even more that she could undo the events of the day. She knew that Rani had other news for her mother which would further add to her burdens. But now her mother was hugging her and crying and all Janki's fears and apprehensions that she would have to listen to another lecture disappeared. She felt a wave of love and concern for her mother and a new understanding of just how hard she worked for them.

Rani and Artie were whispering to each other and Chandi, her first joy at being reunited with daughter now passed, was quick to notice this.

'Artie?'

Artie turned to her. A note fluttered in her hand. 'Ma,' she began, her voice faltering. She held out the piece of paper helplessly.

Chandi took it, her eyes searching Artie's face. What was

wrong? She stared at the piece of paper. Her mind became numb as she absorbed the words.

'Das, Das,' she cried, 'why did you have to do this?'

The piece of paper fell from her hand and was picked up by the wind which carried it away.

Chandi became dizzy. She saw the concerned faces of her daughters as they moved toward her.

Her last conscious thought was that she was swimming in a pool of blood.

CHAPTER SIX

'This is it,' Kunti said, as she pointed to the ramshackle unpainted, wooden hut. She was addressing her son and her long-time acquaintance, Aunt Adee.

Aunt Adee grunted at the sight of the shack, while Jagru stared in disbelief.

'Do you mean people actually live there?' he asked.

'You understand now why I can't let those children stay here all alone tonight,' Kunti said. 'Three girls and a little boy all alone, with their poor mother in hospital. That would never do. God knows where the father is on his political junketings and when he would be back.' She opened the door of the shack and in a practical manner started to pack pieces of clothing and other articles in a large bag she had brought with her.

Jagru was still in shock. He had a received a message at the office that his mother was outside, wanting to talk to him. He would normally have been annoyed — the Secretariat was no place for his mother — but her arrival had given him a welcome excuse to leave the place. It was the 'clean-up' investigation and the threatening proportions it had assumed. Men walked in and out of the department, picking up papers and opening drawers, with great disregard for the fact that they were duplicating each other's actions. Their overwhelming presence enshrouded the place with gloom and uncertainty. His fellow workers were so cowed that no-one made any show of objection to the open suspicions being cast on them. On the contrary, those around him alternatively sat still as if absorbed in their work, or broke out in bursts of simulated activity.

Jagru himself sat still. He was beginning to feel belligerent and put upon. He wasn't going to be railroaded into believing that he had done something wrong. They could go to hell. He was toying with the idea of leaving for the afternoon, when his mother's message came. He picked up his brief case and said to no-one in particular: 'Domestic crisis. I'm going out for a while.'

As he walked through the door, he thought he heard Mitchell murmur: 'Chopping blocks.'

Jagru listened to his mother's story, though his attention wandered at the strange sight of the woman who accompanied her, who appeared to be all pinned up in plastic bags. He had, though, the impression that he'd seen her before. He fell in with his mother's suggestion that they visited the shack where this woman, Chandi, lived. *He* didn't see why the children couldn't stay there for the night, but he didn't voice the thought.

Nothing in his mother's story had prepared him for the sight of the shack. It wasn't even fit for animals. He was as eager now as his mother to get the children away from there. What manner of man was it who allowed his family to live in such a place? But this thought was unworthy. Who was he to judge? He had seen enough of what was happening around the country to know to what pitiable circumstances so many had been reduced. Wasn't that what motivated him — the unbearable sights of the homeless and the hungry? Wasn't that why he had chosen to stay in the country when his degree would have earned him a better job abroad? Wasn't that what all his politicking was about? When his years with his old Party had seemed fruitless, wasn't that why he had taken that giant leap into the tiger's mouth?

He felt a great debt to his mother that she had never allowed him to experience such poverty at first hand. His father had died when he had been far too young to remember him in any great detail. But the way his mother had gone to work in the canefields to ensure his well-being and education was forever imprinted in his mind. If his mother wanted those children to spend the night at his home, it was little to ask. They could bunk down in the spare room.

His mother had finished packing the bag and they began the walk home, the woman in the plastic bags accompanying them. It was getting dark. Street lights were being switched on and, as they reached the corner near their house, they were suddenly bathed in light. The woman's features were sharply illuminated and then Jagru remembered where he had seen her before.

She had been younger, far younger, and she had not been dressed in that monstrous way. How old had he been? Nine? Ten? The scenes slid before his eyes. What had his mother called her. Adelia. That was it. She had been often at their home, helping with the cooking. Snatches of laughter sounded out of the past. She had eventually left to get married, his mother had said and in time he had forgotten about her. He remembered the laughing young woman she had been and found it difficult to reconcile that picture with how she now looked. He turned his face away. What had happened? What had happened to her so that she should have allowed such devastating changes in her life?

They had arrived at his home. Aunt Adee trailed in behind them, without waiting for an invitation. He had thought that the children were at the hospital with their mother. He had not realised that they were already at his home. He had a glimpse of his wife's angry face as he entered.

'Radika,' he said, 'make up the spare room. These children are going to stay here tonight.'

Radika did not move. She glared at him. 'Why? Whose children are they anyway?'

'Oh, don't be foolish, woman,' Jagru said in sudden impatience. 'Have some charity in your heart.'

'Ma,' Radika turned to Kunti, 'you see how your son treating me in front of all these people. He brings these strange children here and lands them on me without an explanation. Am I supposed to do everything he says? Is why he playing stepfather to them?'

Jagru clenched his fist. Sometimes, he felt like hitting her.

Kunti stepped into the breach. 'Jagru had very little to do with it. It was I who brought them here. I surprised at you, Radika. You don't recognise the children of your old friend, Chandi? She collapse by the courts today, you know. She is in hospital now. We can't let these poor, frightened children stay by themselves tonight.'

'I didn't know,' Radika muttered, 'I just come home and find them in the house. Nobody tells me anything.'

'If you were home more often, you would know what was going on,' Jagru said. 'You're out all day and you don't even cook for me any more. You leave my little two-year-old son, your son, in here and if it wasn't for Ma I don't know what would happen.'

'Yes, I know. I know your mother spying on me. That's all she can do,' Radika flared.

'Radika,' Kunti began horrified.

'Don't talk about my mother like that, you —,' he moved towards her threateningly.

Aunt Adee went to stand between them. 'Now, now,' she said, 'you making the little boy cry.' She pointed to Shyam who was beginning to whimper. His three sisters stood with him, huddled in a corner, hardly daring to breathe.

'You're all against me,' Radika flung the words at them. 'I'm not going take this much longer,' and she stormed out of the room.

Jagru passed his hands wearily over his head. He was upset that he had been betrayed into the argument in front of company.

'I sleeping at the market meself or I woulda carry these children home with me,' said Aunt Adee.

'It's okay, Aunt Adee,' Kunti said. 'They'll stay here. Radika'll come around. She's just upset at the moment.'

'They *are* going to stay here,' Jagru said.

'For how long? You na think that poor woman ah go come out a hospital tamorrow, eh?' Aunt Adee asked.

'They'll stay here if I have to —,' Jagru broke off.

Aunt Adee nodded. 'Is what I mean,' she said. 'No sense you go quarrelling with you wife because of them. I know a place where they can go. A nice little house belonging to some people who leaving the country. They trying to rent it. Is going to cost some money, but is a nice place. I know the people. They got good heart. If a big shot person like you talk to them, they be glad to rent the place to you.'

Jagru realised with surprise that she was suggesting he rent a house for these children. Why should he? He was not responsible for them. He had never seen them before in his life. How could they make these claims on him? He was fighting a general battle, not an individual one. He didn't have that kind of money. He saw his mother watching him anxiously. Aunt Adee, a grotesque cap of pinned-up plastic bags overshadowing her face, was hovering around in a dog-like manner, her eyes pleading for a miracle.

Jagru began to feel a little guilty. He thought of his own children. God forbid that they should ever be in such a position. Perhaps he could do it after all. The gesture would please his mother, make her think better of his recent switch. The money could come from the housing allowance which the Secretariat provided him with and which he didn't really need because he had his own house. His salary *was* a generous one, now.

'I'll go see them tomorrow, see what I can fix up.'

Aunt Adee laughed. Even her laughter sounded strange, as if it was cranked up from a deep well, rusty with disuse. 'I got to go now, back to the market,' she said. 'Old folk like me, we can put our heads anywhere for the night. But children, they need a nice place to dream good dreams.'

Kunti was smiling. 'Is a good thing you doing, Jagru. You father woulda been proud of you. You becoming real big.' She turned to the children. 'Poor tired things. You must be starving. I fix you something to eat. Then I show you your room. You'll have nice beds tonight, and tomorrow,' she said with pride, 'tomorrow my son is going to find a nice house for you.'

Radika, sobbing in her room, heard what sounded like laughter and a new wave of resentment washed over her. He seemed to care about all manner of things, but not her. Now he was picking up stray children. Chandi had been her best friend, but school was a long time ago now and she felt no obligation towards her. It was as much as she could do not to tell Chandi, when she came to visit, that she had no great desire to listen to her troubles. Chandi had been the one who always did well at school, while she, Radika, had been the ugly duckling in her shadow. Chandi always got the better marks, was always showered with attention from the other kids and the teachers. She was a schoolmaster's daughter. She could do no wrong. Then when the time came to marry, her father had put on that huge, almost indecently expensive wedding for her. She had a husband. Why didn't he accept his responsibilities? Or why didn't her father take care of them? He'd have done better to have saved his money to dole it out to her in hard times, instead of splashing it all on a big wedding. Now she was being asked to pay the costs of *their* stupidity. At least there couldn't be anything going on between Jagru and Chandi. Her old schoolfriend might have shone more brilliantly than her in those long-ago days, but now Chandi looked faded and worn and older than her years.

Radika felt her own face. She was not getting old. Her resentment boiled up again. Why did he treat her as if he had no use for her any more. Her daughter was young, but growing up quickly. She was noticing things and had made several piercing remarks about Jagru's behaviour. If even his eleven-year-old daughter noticed, who else wouldn't? She wasn't going to take this any longer. He was welcome to his women. There were others who found her attractive and sought her company.

★ ★ ★ ★

'I'm sorry about yesterday,' Asha said. 'After Manu's awful experience, I didn't feel like leaving him alone and the business at the lawyers took such a long time. But we got the best one money can buy.'

'I was busy yesterday, too,' Jagru dismissed the matter, 'trying to rent a house of all things… Is Manu okay?'

Asha waved her hand: 'He's fine. He wasn't beaten or anything like that. But he doesn't feel comfortable in this place anymore. He wants to wrap up the business. Says he'll go and join his wife as soon as the trial is over. He really misses her, you know.'

He hadn't known that Manu's case was going to trial. He thought of telling Asha about the confusion that was going on in the Secretariat with the 'clean-up' campaign, then thought better of it. After all, he didn't really know what was going on and was not mixed up in it, apart from the fact that he was in one of the departments under scrutiny. He was glad that she had not asked him again about his ministerial expectations. He hadn't seen Blair since that first meeting, except distantly in the corridor and the man had seemed too preoccupied to notice him.

'I'm seriously thinking of leaving, too,' said Asha. '...But why are you trying to rent a house?' she laughed. 'I thought you had one.'

Leaving? Would he never see her again?

'Some destitute children,' he stammered. 'Their mother's an old schoolfriend of Radika. She's in hospital and they had no fit place to go.'

How could she leave? Her presence was such a solace when the futility of his efforts mocked him. Why couldn't he tell her what she meant to him. Ten, eleven years difference. What was that?

The waiter hovered at the table. 'Sir and madam ready to order?' he asked with hushed respect. It was a good restaurant, one of the best. He wouldn't have asked Asha to meet him anywhere less splendid. He placed the orders.

'Is Radika joining us?' Asha asked.

Radika, Radika. She was suddenly there, very much between them, her shadowy presence curdling the moment.

'I seem to bump into her wherever I go these days,' she continued. 'I could have sworn that I saw her just as I was coming into the restaurant. Of course, I might have been mistaken. It might have been someone who looked very much like her.'

Jagru sweated and shifted uncomfortably. What was Radika up to? He had planned to turn up to Asha's birthday dinner alone — Radika would be unwell or something like that. Now he saw a better excuse.

'I'm afraid she's very busy for the big party we're planning. She said to give you her excuses for tonight. She won't be able to make it. But I'll come,' he added with a nervous laugh.

How could she leave? But he had to keep on talking.

'You're probably bumping into her all over the place because she's been doing a lot of shopping, you know, for this party.'

The arrival of the waiter with the main course covered the slight silence which ensued. Fish baked in creole sauce and served in Spanish rice.

'Smells delicious,' Asha said, as she picked up her fork. In between mouthfuls, she asked: 'What was it you wanted to see me about?'

Jagru hurriedly gulped down a piece of fish. He'd almost forgotten the pretext under which he had invited her to lunch.

'A matter I was having some difficulty with. I thought you might have been able to help. It's all over now,' he said inventing and resolving the problem all in one sentence.

He thought he saw a flicker of doubt on Asha's face. He had an inspiration. He pushed his hand in his pocket to bring out the little box which he had been itching to show her from the start.

'Actually it was to ask what you wanted for your birthday. I didn't want to wait until the actual date. I had a little help from the girl at the place where I bought it. I hope you like it... Happy birthday,' he said, presenting it to her.

Asha extended her hand. She liked receiving presents. She opened the box.

The waiter was at her elbow: 'Everything satisfactory, Madam?'

Asha inclined her head. She pressed the catch on the box. A magnificent bracelet lay within. Her pleasure faded. It was too expensive.

'I can't,' she said.

Jagru protested: 'I wish you would accept it. It can't really compare with your friendship to me these past months. It's helped a lot. Things haven't always been bright with me and Radika, you know.'

There, now, he had said it. At least he had gone a little further to give her an inkling of his feelings.

Asha hesitated, then decided to accept the box. A silence enveloped the table. She began to eat hurriedly. She was a fool. Radika had been following her. Was she collecting evidence for a divorce? She didn't want any part of this. Jagru was a good friend, but she didn't want anything more from him. Or was she imagining that he wanted more, reading too much into the gift?

Jagru was brooding over the news of her imminent departure from the country. Why did the things he wanted in life always elude him?

'When are you going?' he asked abruptly.

'Where?' Asha, caught up in her own thoughts, was lost.

'Out of the country,' Jagru stumbled.

'Oh *that*.'

Jagru winced. The casual air cut deeply.

'As soon as my papers come through. I'm waiting for a reply from the college, you know, where Delia is attending. I guess after they accept me, things will go pretty quickly.'

Jagru could see her already on the plane, out of his life.

'You'll let me know what's happening, keep me posted?' The words came out in an anxious rush.

'Of course,' said Asha. She got up quickly. 'I've got to go,' she said, 'or else there'll be no dinner tonight. Thanks very much for a delightful lunch...' She hesitated, ' and for the bracelet.'

Jagru stood up. 'I really enjoyed it.' He held onto her hand. 'Asha...' he said. He found it difficult to continue. He watched her walk away, saw the heads turned to observe her. A woman of beauty. She was tantalising: the way she brightened his life, and now she was leaving, going out of his life for ever. How could he stop her? Try to capture her heart? Could he embark on a new love, fresh feelings? There were so many past commitments and present confusions in his life. His wife. His mother. His beliefs. The demands of his conscience. What could he offer this woman?

★ ★ ★ ★

Chandi knew when the child went. She noted its passing as if she was a stranger, standing apart from her body to observe its antics as if it was some newly-discovered species. Her children, Artie, Janki and Rani: all looking concerned. And that nice woman from the market. And Kunti, Radika's mother-in-law, who had been such a good friend when she really needed help. Where was Das? Had she heard them say that he had gone to get medicine for her? She thought she spoke to Artie, to tell her that Shyam mustn't cry, that everything would be all right. But they didn't seem to hear her. She couldn't make them hear her. She thought her husband was somewhere in the room, but she couldn't see him. Everything was so hazy. She drifted off. Where was she? She thought she had been in a hospital. But that could not be. No tube was wrapped on her arm, pressing her skin down. She was not lying on a bed. She could walk, move. She could hear music and people laughing and talking around her. They all wanted to talk to her and to shake her hand. She could see her father and he was smiling and laughing too and all dressed up. She, too, had on fineries, with a big necklace and bangles making her hand heavy. She clapped her hands. They were going to a wedding. No, they were at a wedding. It was her wedding. She was getting married. And there was Lal coming into the yard, his silk clothes shining in the sunlight, bringing a great number of people in train. She started to rush toward him, to greet him as she had always done. But someone held her back, laughingly. She had to be the demure bride, waiting for the rites to be performed, when she would say her vows before the sacred fire and garland her life partner. Chandi watched him come with his proud procession, looking like a king. But then his nice new clothes disappeared. He was sitting on a bed, thin and worried and his face years older. It was a hospital bed and she was there with him, trying to talk to him. Only he wouldn't talk to her. But now he was no longer on the bed. She was lying there. But she was not ill, but relaxed and pleased with herself. An effortless labour. She had hardly felt anything. And now, here was little Shyam, nestling in the nook of her arm, his face rosy and everybody saying what a fine-looking baby he was. But this wasn't Shyam she was holding. This baby didn't have a face. It was half-formed, a poor shrivelled-up thing. This wasn't her baby. She cried out in horror.

'My baby,' she said, 'my baby.'

Chandi became aware of voices. A man in white held her hand and was speaking to her in a soothing manner.

'It's going to be all right,' he said. 'Everything's going to be all right.'

Other faces were looking down at her, smiling encouragingly. Where were her children? Where was Das? Knowledge returned to her slowly. She had lost her child. She had lost Das, too. He had gone away without telling her. Gone to a job across the border, so that he could earn money for her. What did she want with such money? Her son. What dangers had he gone to face for her sake? Tears trickled down her cheeks.

'There now,' the doctor said, 'you mustn't upset yourself. 'Nurse!' he called.

Chandi felt the needle prick her arm and she slipped into a welcoming nothingness.

'She's going to be all right,' the doctor said. 'But keep an eye on her.' He shook his head. 'She wouldn't have been able to carry the child all the way. Under too much stress... Well, who am I to see next?'

She must have slept a long time. When she woke she felt refreshed, with a lightness about her heart. Her children were around her bedside and Artie was telling her about the new house, with its nice beds and furniture, which they now had.

'Uncle Jagru gave it to us,' said Artie. 'He's having a party Saturday. He says Rani can take Shyam with her to babysit his little son and that Janki and I could help out in the kitchen. So don't worry, Ma, we're managing all right. Just get better.'

Chandi was not worrying. She felt an extraordinary calm and a remoteness from everything.

'Your father came home?' she asked.

Artie shook her head. 'I went to that place where they keep meetings and a woman there said he had gone out of town to speak at a rally.'

Chandi said: 'You mustn't go back there.' She shook her head. Politics. He wouldn't listen.

Shyam burst in on her thoughts. 'Ma, we have a nice new house. When Dad sees it, he won't go away again. He'll stay and play with me.'

Janki said anxiously: 'Ma, you'll come home soon? I'll stay home and help out, so you won't have to work so hard.'

'Auntie Kunti said she knows someone who might get me a job,' said Artie. 'She says it's a secretary job and the pay is good.'

Chandi did not have the will to protest at her daughter leaving school. She struggled with the words: 'Why is Radika's husband paying for the house?'

'They're very kind. They've been very kind to us,' said Artie. 'He said he's going to help until things get better. He said...' She had been going to tell her mother how kind Jagru and Kunti had been about Janki's matter, how they had gone to see the people at the store, and the man at the police station. She remembered how the woman at the store had fawned over them and had agreed to take the envelope from Kunti to drop the matter. She could have told her mother how the man at the station had been very respectful, had kept saying 'Sir' to Jagru. They had all acted as if he was someone very important and if they didn't behave properly, they might be in trouble over their jobs. But Artie wasn't too sure she should tell her mother any of this. She didn't want to upset her all over again, by reminding her of the shoplifting incident.

'They're very nice people,' she repeated earnestly.

Chandi shook her head, as if to dispel some fog of unreality. 'Nothing happens for nothing,' she said. At least nothing good ever did.

A nurse stopped by her bedside. 'Just a few more days,

Mrs. Panday and we'll have you out of here, strong and fit again.' She turned to the children. 'Remarkably strong, your mother, for all that she looks so fragile.'

But she was fragile, thought Jagru, who at his mother's insistence had accompanied her to the hospital, and had just arrived. He had only met Chandi once before when she had been another indistinct blur in the sea of faces at his wedding celebrations. Wedding celebrations! What a laugh. Chandi, with her tragic, vulnerable eyes, was so different from Radika, who so often these days looked surly and sour. He felt touched by that vulnerability. Here was someone who needed him, one of the trampled masses he could use his power to help.

'My son, Jagru,' he heard his mother saying proudly to the woman on the bed.

Jagru hovered awkwardly after muttering 'hello', embarrassed by the fulsome expressions of gratitude. He felt an impostor, masquerading under the guise of kindness. He'd just been trying to please his mother, to satisfy his own conscience and to stifle the voice inside which said all his efforts were useless, a sham. What was it all: a plush office, an empty job, fancy rhetoric. What was real was the suffering of this woman lying on the bed with her hollow eyes, her face telling of the wreckage of human hopes and dreams.

He became aware that the time had run out. Visitors were being ushered out of the ward.

His mother said: 'My son got to go to work now. But if he get the chance, he gon come and see you again. He a good man, my son. His heart's in the right place.'

Jagru responded sheepishly to their smiles of gratitude and hurried out into the sunshine, leaving his mother to have her final chat.

Too much soul-searching, he thought. Too much digging into the maggots of doubt in his mind. He tried to shake off his gloom, but the woman on the bed haunted his thoughts. What right had he to such different fortunes? These thoughts weren't getting him anywhere, but then, thinking about Asha was even worse. She was a wisp, intangible; she had never really been in his life, but thoughts of her departure plunged him into even deeper depression. What was life with Radika? A confining misery, an emptiness broken only by their incessant quarrels. She had grown sour ever since he had thrown cold water on her urgings that they should leave the country, to accept her mother's invitation to join her. Why couldn't she accept his work was here? She had even begun to accuse him of all kinds of ulterior motives for wanting to stay. When she was not quarrelling, she was so cold these days. In the early days of their marriage she had driven him away with her expectations, no, her relentless demands for protestations of love and platitudes of devotion. She had stifled him. Now she was acting as if he had done her some great wrong. She was sadly mistaken if she thought that he would be the one to effect peace between them, to even deny the acts of unfaithfulness she obviously thought he was committing. She had no right to be leaving the home so often. He was the breadwinner, not she. Why couldn't she behave like a good wife? She had no right to go around harassing his friends. Particularly Asha. He had taxed her about this when his softer words had failed to make any impact on her. He had described her shadowing games as the silly fears of a neurotic middle-aged woman. This had provoked fury. Her words still rang in his ears.

'Silly middle-aged!' she screamed. 'Silly middle-aged! You think I care what you do with yourself. You think you're a real big shot, eh, with your fancy job and your fancy woman? But just wait. Wait and see who has the last laugh.'

'Radika,' he had said, 'Why don't you stop it? Why don't you try to behave like an adult? Stop all these insane attempts to hurt me and do something concrete to make our marriage work.'

'I like that,' she raged. 'Do something to make our marriage work. Has Mr Big Shot ever tried to do anything? You come home and I'm here waiting like a doormat to greet you. You don't tell me anything. You don't act like you want to see me. You leave the house at every opportunity and now you want to put all the blame on me.' She had begun to cry violently.

On this occasion he had ended the battle of words and had made some attempt to soothe her by steering her thoughts to the party they were planning. Many important people had accepted invitations — although PM Rouche had not given any indication whether he would come, but then everybody knew that he was ailing. Even so, the evening had all the makings of being very successful. There would be other such evenings, and who knew how many invitations they would receive in return.

This subject was evidently fruitful territory, for Radika, after a thoughtful silence, had gradually allowed herself to be placated. This was fortunate. He could not have afforded a sullen wife at the party.

These thoughts carried him back to the office and other concerns. When was this damn investigation going to end?

If they were going to arrest anyone, why didn't they do it and let the place get back to what passed for normality? He was tired of seeing men in dark clothes wandering about with their disconcerting aimlessness.

He frowned as he saw Gordon Brown, the man who had proclaimed himself to be in charge of the investigation, sitting at his desk.

'Ah. Mr Persaud, the very man I want to see. Glad to see you're an early worm. Ha, ha. I meant early bird.'

Jagru was not amused. Why was the man always hailing him in that familiar way. What did he want with him? He didn't know anything about anyone. What could he know, so lately arrived? He was getting tired of all this.

He tried to hide his displeasure. 'What can I do for you?' He saw John Tyler watching them from behind the cover of a magazine to which he seemed glued.

Gordon Brown rubbed his hands. 'A lot man, a lot,' he said. 'I keep telling them to give me an assistant.'

Jagru stiffened, but Brown did not seem to notice.

'Actually, it's about this party you're giving. I know you meant to include me…'

Jagru was disgusted and at the same time relieved.

'Of course, you're on the list. I'm afraid we're behind with sending out some of the invitations. These things catch up with one.'

Brown got up to allow Jagru to seat himself. He slapped him on the back. 'Well, see you there then,' he said. 'That's if I don't have some reason to see you before. Ha-ha.'

Mitchell came across on the pretext of borrowing a file. He kept his voice low. 'I shouldn't really be talking to you,' he said, ' even passing notes is getting risky these days— Evidence… What did he want?'

Jagru was inclined to laugh as he told how the man had cadged the invitation, but he was a little flattered too.

Mitchell immediately became morose. 'Brown wanting to come to your party,' he muttered. 'I wonder if I ought not to come, after all.' He hurried away when he saw Brown returning.

'I forgot to give you this,' he said, offering an envelope he had in his hand.

Jagru took it with some trepidation. He shook himself mentally. He was becoming as paranoid as Mitchell. He caught Tyler watching him intensely; the man gave him a sickly smile and turned his eyes away.

Jagru almost ripped the envelope open. There was a brief note inside.

I would like to see you as soon as possible. It was from Carl Blair.

His heart pounding, Jagru got up. It could mean anything. But he hoped it would mean only one thing. He had to knock several times at Blair's door before a voice irritably informed him that the door was open. The woman at the desk wanted to know his business. She waved him to a seat and picked up the telephone.

Why was she whispering into the phone? His wanting to see Blair wasn't a state secret, was it? Everyone seemed to be making a career out of acting peculiarly.

He seemed to be waiting for a long time after she had finished her call. He began to fidget. The man had said that he wanted to see him as soon as possible.

The wait became interminable.

Eventually, the door to the inner office opened and Carl Blair came out. He looked pleased with himself and was smiling.

'All in the bag, Molly, all in the bag,' he said to his secretary, winking at her. To Jagru's surprise, Molly winked back.

Blair turned to him: 'Ah Mr Persaud, you waited. Good. Step in.'

Inside the office, Jagru was kept waiting for several minutes before Blair invited him to sit.

'Your function Saturday, is it still on?'

Jagru stared, but recovered enough to nod. What did his party have to do with anything?

'Interesting things, these functions,' Blair said; 'they often get enough important people together to turn out to be real conferences. More business done at a party than in an office,' he added.

Jagru couldn't see where all this was leading.

Blair had fallen silent. He seemed to be thinking deeply. Finally, he asked: 'What do you think about this clean-up investigation we've launched?'

Jagru felt his way cautiously. 'It's always good to have an organisation with people you can trust.'

Blair leaned forward. He was suddenly enthusiastic. 'I like that. Very good. That's the key word. Trust. You're quite right.' He added: 'We need people we can *trust*. People who won't constantly *undermine* this administration and all our efforts to have a better place for *everyone* to live.'

Jagru said quietly: 'If we can do that, Sir, it would be wonderful. It's something I feel strongly about, the welfare of others and I would be pleased to be given the opportunity to help, in any way I could.'

'No need to tell me that,' Blair pointed to a folder before him. 'I've got your file here. I know how committed you are. This investigation is going to have its impact — we're going to lose men.' He added quickly, as if afraid Jagru would misinterpret him: 'Don't get me wrong. It's very necessary to show the public that we're serious about reform. But if we're going to maintain our level of efficiency, we need a hard core of men in the right place, men who will keep the fabric of this Secretariat together. I hope you understand what I'm saying.'

Jagru said eagerly: 'I'm willing to contribute in any way I can. All I want is to contribute to the best of my ability.'

'Yes, yes.' Blair seemed impatient that he had been interrupted. 'I just wanted to alert you. I may call upon you anytime. In fact, very soon now.' He seemed to brood once again.

Jagru nodded, not rushing into words this time. He was learning.

'Well, that's all for now,' Blair dismissed him, 'I'll see you later.'

As Jagru turned to go, Blair said: 'Have you been assigned a car yet?'

Jagru shook his head. No mention had been made of a car in the letter — the only one he had received — although his several superfluous allowances had included one for a maid.

'We'll see. We'll see,' said Blair. 'Well so long. I'll see if I can look in on that party of yours.'

Jagru was already out of the door. He did not know how to review the conversation. Some notice was being taken of him at last, but he had an uneasy feeling that he was being manoeuvred into the investigation. Why couldn't they give him some real work? But there was some hope in his step as he went back to his department. The recognition was a little belated, but it was coming. It was going to come.

That night, Jagru went home to dream. He dreamt of his party. He had a confused picture of shaking hands almost constantly. Many of them were people from the Secretariat. But then the faces seemed to change and he saw that he was looking at his old colleagues. Dada and Paul Bagat and Garth among others. He had not invited them. He could not understand why they had come. He wanted to tell them to leave. But when he tried to tell them this, the words wouldn't come. They glided away to talk to his wife, who seemed to be on the most intimate terms with them, and soon all their faces, including Radika's, were turned towards him and they were all laughing as if they shared a huge joke.

Then their images disappeared and he saw Asha and he was moving toward her to tell her of the strange things he had imagined. But then he saw that she was dancing with Carl Blair and didn't seem to want to talk to him. Over his shoulder, Blair said, 'Good man, good man. We'll soon have you in the right place.' 'Is this the right place?' a voice said at the door and he recognised Chandi, dressed in rags and pointing an accusing finger at him. The images disappeared and he was in a strange place all alone. He heard a voice which he recognised as his mother's, but he could not see her and he began to panic. He began to run and found himself on an unfamiliar road which seemed to stretch for miles and miles without end. His feet were still running, but he was not moving from the spot. He could not move. He made a great effort and awoke to find himself tangled up in the bedsheets.

He must have been making a good deal of noise, for Radika was sitting up at her side of the bed, glaring at him.

CHAPTER SEVEN

As it was, Jagru's fears were unfounded. Not only did his unwanted former colleagues not materialise, but also many of the bigwigs he had invited put in an appearance, including Carl Blair and Secretariat Head, A.D. James. His one disappointment was Asha. She rang at the last minute to say that she had got caught up in a business matter and might not be able to tear herself away in time.

'Come if you can,' Jagru urged; 'it doesn't matter if you're late.' As much as to win friends at the Secretariat, the party was intended to impress Asha, and the thought that she might not make it cast a gloom on the evening. After a while, though, he was pulled into the spirit of things as he saw how well the party was going, hearing the lively hum of conversation mixed with laughter and the clinking of glasses. He was above all both flattered and bewildered by the attention he was receiving from the 'big' men. A.D. James and several of the ministers all took time to chat with him, as if they were on easy terms of intimacy, while Blair constantly hovered, making comments calculated to please him.

'You've got a lovely home,' he said, 'and a beautiful wife to go with it.' He seemed to want to say more, but stopped, though Jagru saw his eyes keep straying to Radika, who kept her distance at the other end of the room.

Jagru had to admit she looked stunning, although he felt a little uncomfortable about the plunging neckline of her dress and suspected that the men gathered around her were there more for the view than for the scintillating conversation.

He shrugged. She was enjoying herself. Why should he care that she put on a show? His mother, he knew, had raised disapproving eyebrows. Kunti herself was clad in a dress which covered her ankles as well as her arms and, in the custom of Indian women of her generation, her head was covered with an orhani. She looked happy, glad for her son that the party was going so successfully. And, apart from James Mitchell who wandered around with a long face, everyone seemed happy.

Jagru remained puzzled by the attention focussed on him. Why was A.D. James, whom he had met only distantly in the corridor, making such a fuss of him? He had felt then that James had no great desire to meet him, but now the man was positively effusive. James had arrived with his wife, loudly expressed his pleasure at the invitation and kept returning to Jagru's corner with some facetious comment or other. At one point, he poured into Jagru's ears a lewd story about Gordon Brown and his adventures with a waitress.

'Our Mr. Gordon Brown is not so clean himself,' he chuckled. He seemed to delight in disparaging Brown. Jagru listened politely, making sure he gave away no indication of his feelings, wondering, though, why men in such high positions took so much pleasure in dirty, sordid little stories. He felt that all the attention had to be significant. These men were in a position to know what was happening. Some, indeed, were the decision-makers, and there were enough of them in his house for the highest council to convene. He was pleased that both Carl Blair and A.D. James were present. If anyone knew what was happening, they did. It was they who oversaw the press releases and, of course, they were always closeted with Rouche. Perhaps, too, now that the

P M was so constantly indisposed, they had more influence than ever. Was an announcement about his future going to be made at the party? Whose place would *he* fill? Who had fallen into disfavour lately? Of course, there might be no need to follow the customary practice of demoting someone. A new portfolio might be created for him. It would not be the first time a position was specially created.

He saw his daughter coming across the room towards him. She walked a little stiffly, very conscious, it seemed, of her position as Daddy's daughter. She was dressed very simply and he was glad he had won on that point with Radika. She had wanted to bedeck the girl, dress her like the young woman she would soon, but had not yet, become. She was still a child and there was no need to push her into adulthood before the time came.

James had suddenly reappeared at his elbow. 'Lovely girl you've got there,' he said. 'Was talking to her a few minutes earlier. Seems very sensible. Looks like she could do just as well as her father when the times comes. Which school is she attending?'

Jagru told him.

James nodded. 'Good school. Good to start them right from the beginning... No trouble getting her a place there, I hope.'

Jagru hesitated, his face flushed. He was saved from answering by Bharka's arrival.

Bharka smiled brightly at James as she tiptoed to whisper in her father's ear, 'Phone for you.'

Jagru made his excuses, but James said: 'I should be leaving. Time to leave. A habit of mine. I never stay too long at any party. Wouldn't do, would it. Although yours is such an interesting one. I should really make an exception this time. To watch the fireworks.'

Jagru was puzzled. What fireworks? But before he could question James, the man was moving to detach his wife from a group. He returned their wave as they went through the door. Fireworks? What did James mean? Was there really going to be an announcement then? The phone. He had almost forgotten the call. He slowly eased himself out of the room.

Blair stopped him as he went. 'Not leaving so soon, man, are you? Just when the party is going to liven up.' He seemed highly amused at his joke.

Jagru mumbled a suitable excuse as he went to the phone.

'Hello, hello, hello, hello.'

Silence on the other end. Jagru listened for a while, but all he could hear was a slight, buzzing sound. The caller must have been cut off. He replaced the receiver and decided to wait. Who could have been calling him? He sat for about five minutes. Had it been Asha? As the minutes went by, he convinced himself that it had been and that she was having difficulty getting through.

His hand hovered over the phone. Should he call her? Would she not think it odd that he was calling her in the middle of his own social gathering? But suppose she had been trying to call him because she needed some kind of help. His hand connected with the phone. At least he had a legitimate excuse. Someone had called, had tried to call him.

She seemed surprised to hear his voice, but not annoyed. No, she had not called him. No, she would not be able to make the party anymore. Her voice sounded genuinely regretful. Jagru hoped that there was no serious problem. Was it anything he could help with? He heard the hesitation in her voice. Not really. It was to do with their travelling plans and the acquisition of visas. She changed the subject. She hoped the party was going well. They chatted of inconsequential matters.

So she really meant to leave. He sank into the chair to pursue his gloomy thoughts, but something nagged at him. The party. Why was everything so suddenly quiet? He got up from the chair. As he did, he saw Radika behind him. How long had she been standing there? Her face was suffused with anger.

'Can't keep away, can you?' she hissed. 'Can't keep away from your fancy piece even in the middle of your party. Well, you better go and see what's happening to your precious party. Not much of a party left, I should think!' She flounced away. Jagru hurried after her. Why had the place gone silent? A lone voice broke into the silence. A man sounded as if he was at a rally, making a speech. It was Brown. Where did he think he was?

★ ★ ★ ★

Asha hung up the phone, feeling glad that the excuse she had given Jagru about not attending the party was true. Manu and Bulu had immediately opted out by pleading work when Jagru had made the invitation to them at her birthday dinner. But he had pressed her so much and had been so insistent, that she had not known how to refuse and in the end had promised to attend, though she had always known she would not go. She didn't need Manu to tell her how crazy it would be to show their faces while the hunt was on for traders and the Special Squad was having fun, levelling charges and accusations all over the place. Their friend from the Secretariat would be there and it would be difficult to avoid talking to him. Wasn't Jagru being a bit naive, inviting them when he knew the kind of business they were in? She had heard that the campaign started at the very top and that the Secretariat itself was under scrutiny. They would no doubt be looking for scapegoats, though she suspected that Jagru himself would be protected; not to do so would be to under-exploit his value.

She shook her head as she returned to the sitting room. The call had not been important. She, Bulu and Manu had been engaged in a heated discussion, revolving around a visitor, a man who had visas to sell.

Asha considered the whole idea preposterous. Their visitor was a conman who was just trying to swindle them out of a hunk of cash. She had not *said* this, but implied it by her vehement opposition to the idea. Why was Manu trying to buy a visa? He had enough assets and cash to convince the visa people of his bona fides. She had heard that if you had money, real money, there were countries, free countries, which welcomed you with open arms.

She was glad when the visitor took his leave. He would call later, he said, to hear their decision.

'Don't bother,' Asha thought, though she didn't voice the words as she ushered the man out. Now she would speak her mind.

Manu forestalled her. 'I don't see what we've got to lose, Asha. The money's unimportant and it's worth a try. I hear they giving you such a hassle these days when you go through the right channels. You have to wait for ages. I don't want to stay here any longer. I want to take my children and get out of this damn place as quickly as I can.'

'I agree with Manu,' said Bulu, 'I think it's worth a try.' Bulu was the youngest of the three and he often agreed with Manu.

'Well just suppose, he's able to get visas. He goes and tries to buy yours. What happens then? Think of what can happen if the wrong people find out what you're trying to do?' she argued.

'I've got to try, Asha,' Manu said wearily, 'I'm tired of it all here. I want to get away as quickly as I can to be with Delia. If I can leave even before the trial…'

'But why does he want the money before?' Asha asked. 'Surely if he's on the level, he can trust us to give it to him afterwards.'

'He says that in the line of business he's in, he can't afford to trust anyone,' Manu said doggedly. 'You heard him yourself. And I can well believe that. If we can't trust him, why should he trust us? I want to get away. Who knows when this trial will be over. I know someone who's been going to court for years over the most trivial matter — and he can't leave the country while the case going on — at least not permanently.'

Bulu said: 'I hear they trying to speed up things with this extra court they forming. It might go quickly after all.'

'They trying to kill the country, man, cutting off its lifeline by harassing the traders,' said Manu. He shuddered. 'I hear they might even jail a few.'

Asha understood Manu's fears. No, doubt, she would have felt the same way if she had gone through his experience at the hands of the Special Squad — and Manu had a family to worry about.

'I still think you shouldn't give this man any money for a visa. I don't believe he can do anything.'

'Don't press me on this, Asha, I've got to try,' Manu said, 'just for me and the kids. You and Bulu can afford to wait. I can't.'

★ ★ ★ ★

Jagru moved angrily towards Brown, but was immobilised by what he heard.

'Of course, we were very glad to have Mr Persaud's help. As you know, he's a very important man in the Secretariat who's destined for higher things. He agreed with me that we had to go through with this public unmasking. The saboteurs in our midst have to understand that not only will they no longer be tolerated, but they must also know that they will be shamed and humiliated publicly. We will no longer accept their insidious practices.'

Who? What? He agree with Brown? Was Brown mad? What was he talking about? John Tyler seemed to be in the middle of it. Now Tyler burst in angrily on Brown's speech.

'You can't do this. You're infringing my constitutional rights. I'm entitled to a fair hearing. I'm entitled to be considered innocent until proven otherwise.' Tyler was on the verge of hysteria.

Jagru realised that Tyler's hands were handcuffed. Why did they have to disrupt his party by making these infantile arrests? How dare they suggest that he was involved in the entire scheme? But he kept quiet.

Brown's voice was raised once more. 'Nonsense! How can you suggest that we're tampering with your constitutional rights. You know very well that the very word 'constitution' is sacred to us. As for claiming that you won't be given a fair trial, that's insulting rubbish. Nobody here has said you're a guilty man, eh. Come on, tell us. Has anybody done that?' he goaded.

John Tyler pushed his hands out. 'What are these?' he asked sullenly.

'Why handcuffs, man, handcuffs. You use them when you make an arrest, you know. We have evidence to make charges against you and sufficient reason to believe that if we didn't do it immediately, we wouldn't be given the chance again. We...'

'That's a lie. You knew very well I would be at work on Monday,' Tyler cried out.

'John Tyler, I must advise you to be careful of what you say. You are under arrest and your rights have been read to you. For the information of these good people here, you'll be held until and if bail is given and you'll be put on trial in a court of law. I did not call you guilty. I was merely speaking out against a group of saboteurs who aid corruption. I only allege that you belong to this group. I don't pronounce sentence. So please get your facts straight. I've been very patient explaining myself. I hope you remember that. You can take him away,' he said to the two men who had materialised next to him.

'Friends,' he waved his arms encouragingly, 'please resume your enjoyment. I know you will all understand the need for us to make this arrest so public. It's the only way we can flush out corruption.'

The talk resumed slowly, almost in whispers. People began to take their leave in embarrassed shuffles. Jagru could feel the tension still thickening the atmosphere.

His mother came to stand next to him. He felt the sympathy of her presence and wanted bury his head in her arms, to assuage his tiredness and frustration. How did one deal with such people? This was his living room. Why were they trying to spread their sickness within it? His official life had nothing to do with his home and family. How could they upset his mother this way? Was nothing dear to them? Was this the price he had to pay, be seen as part and parcel of such vulgar antics?

Brown strolled over to him. He seemed jubilant, rubbing his hands. 'We've got off to a good start, man. We'll soon have people begging to make confessions. Oh, yes, we'll soon have the Secretariat cleaned up and ready to start again.'

He lowered his voice to a confidential level. 'Tyler was small time, of course, taking bribes and things like that. We're after a really big one. But I shouldn't really be telling you more as yet, even though you're assisting me. Information on a need to know basis, eh,' he laughed raucously.

Had he been assisting him? Jagru wondered who had lured him away with the telephone call. But why did they have to use his living room? If they wanted publicity so badly, why hadn't they put it in the papers, the way they did everything else. He supposed it was a question of who their public was. Tactics had to be changed when dealing with your own.

More people were leaving. His mother was sitting down. Bharka had retired from the party on his instructions. Radika still seemed to be having fun and was carrying on a vivacious conversation with a couple.

Blair came to bid him goodnight, a smile playing around his lips. 'Our Mr Brown is very spectacular in his methods, eh? But if it achieves results, what can one say? The important thing is to have it all over so that we can get on with our jobs, eh? Thanks for your cooperation,' he added, as he took his leave.

Jagru remained silent. What could he say? He hadn't wanted any part of it. But the thing was done. There was no point in any protest. But was this what he had changed parties for, to be involved in this kind of mess? What exactly *was* he involved in?

★ ★ ★ ★

Ban threw down the newspaper. 'Such utter rubbish they try to make you believe these days. Now they trying to push this clean-up campaign down our throats to take the public's mind off the general state of affairs. But will the people be fooled? They'll ask, "Will this campaign give us anything to eat?"'

'I hear they start making arrests,' said Lal Panday, as he busily scribbled on a piece of paper, preparing one of his speeches.

'Small fry,' said Ban. 'You don't change the tires of a car if the engine is bad.'

Lal Panday did not reply, but continued to scribble in furious dedication.

Mitzi came through the door. She was devoted to Ban and did not share the view of Ban's former colleagues that Ban was as crazy as a bat. She saw beyond Ban's hard exterior, developed as the survivor of the many prisons she had been hauled in and out of and the frequent clashes she had with the authorities. She had known Ban when she had been with the other side, when her sympathies had lain elsewhere. Ban had celebrated with the Official Party after their rigged victory, believing in their claims that they would strive for development and prosperity. But she had soon become disillusioned by their total absence of principle and the sanctioning of activities which helped only a privileged few and added to the burdens of the general public. She had worked with Ban during this period and had followed her transformation each step of the way, sharing Ban's confidences, understanding how troubled she had been when she saw how men were being placed in positions for which they were ill-equipped. What treacherous form of patronage was this? The corruption Ban feared had manifested itself. Ban could not live within such a system and had left to become one of the founders of the Workers Party, and Mitzi, loyal to the last, had followed her.

Now, coming into the room, Mitzi was greeted by one of

Ban's customarily abrupt instructions.

'A tape on your desk. Needs transcribing.'

Mitzi moved quickly to work, as always admiring Ban's tireless energy. Ban had always been like that, rare in her commitment even amongst those who shared her objectives. That was why the struggle was so hard. There were so many who did not care enough, so few who wanted to get involved. They were so busy trying to make ends meet that they had no time for any other considerations, political or otherwise.

But Lal Panday was different. Mitzi thought guiltily of the messages she had on her desk for him. She planned to give them to him. Of course, she would. She was just waiting for an appropriate moment when she would not disturb what he was doing by other considerations.

'How's it going?' The question came from Ban as she peered over Lal's shoulder at his speech-writing efforts. Mitzi had gone to sit at her desk to transcribe the tape. Ban began to read the pages which Lal had finished, admiring his single-mindedness. They had a lot in common even though their ancestors had come from different continents. From the moment she had seen Lal Panday, she had known he was different. There were few who were able to sacrifice their family life for the cause. The question had never arisen for her because she had no family. But Lal was a family man who knew at first hand hunger and deprivation — a grass-roots person like herself. Physical hunger was not the only kind he knew. He had a different kind of hunger and Ban, recognising this hunger in him, found that he made a perfect speaker at their rallies. She congratulated him now on the speech he had just written. Mitzi, watching them, understood their rapport.

They were both people who had made tremendous sacrifices in their different ways. Mitzi felt uneasy that Lal had abandoned his family and left them to fend for themselves, but it was all toward a greater cause. She wished that there was some sort of wage he could be paid, but as account keeper, among other things, she knew that there was no money. The little that trickled in hardly sufficed to keep the organisation going.

Ban was speaking to Lal again. She listened idly to their words above the noise of the tape recording.

'Did you find out where they'd gone?'

'Who?' Lal questioned in turn. 'Oh, them. Probably over the river. Chandi must have gone to her father. I told her to go before. I don't know why she didn't.' He dismissed the question.

Mitzi felt that she should speak now, give him the messages she had received. But perhaps she had left them for too long. She kept silent, not knowing what to do.

'I think we'll have a good turnout tonight,' Lal said. 'I'll go see the man about the seats.'

He had gone before Mitzi could make up her mind whether to tell him anything.

Ban passed by her desk with a huge book in her hand. 'I'm going to check out this new court. See what they make of this campaign. It'll be funny to see some of those gentlemen in the dock.'

★ ★ ★

Kunti carefully packed the bags with Chandi's few belongings from the cupboard near her bed. 'Everything in now. My son's going to be here in another few minutes with his nice new car.' The statement lacked its usual pride. She still hadn't recovered from the incident at the party and she had misgivings about the new position her son had been given at the Secretariat, even though a big car had come with it.

'Ma, I'm not sure I like what's going on,' he had said. 'This is not quite what I expected when I decided to join the Secretariat. I don't like being mixed up in all of this, but I can't really back out now. If I gave up, what would there be left for me to do?'

Kunti hadn't known what to reply. She knew her son. He had a strong instinct for self-preservation, but he would not deliberately try to harm anyone. The problem with his wife: that was a different matter. But he had a conscience about things. He meant well. He wanted to help people. She sighed.

Chandi said: 'I can't thank you and your son enough, and Radika...'

'Jagru is just doing his duty,' Kunti said brusquely. She had grown to like Chandi, to admire the way she faced up to things and to realise that they were alike in at least one respect. Chandi bore a great love for her children. Kunti was pleased to help and had taken great pleasure in bringing Chandi the news that Artie had won the job as secretary with a businessman whom Jagru knew. At least Chandi would not feel that she needed to go to work immediately at the market. She owed it to herself and her family to rest and build up her strength.

'Here comes Jagru,' Chandi said.

Jagru smiled at the two women. There was a real affinity between them, he thought. Chandi seemed to have such a calming, soothing aura about her, as if she was able to appreciate others' problems and knew how to listen and to sympathise. Jagru laughed silently at his fancies. Of course she understood people's problems. She had enough of her own, didn't she?

He himself was in an uncertain mood. The car had come as a nice surprise, but when he had learnt what the promotion meant, his pleasure had evaporated.

'We want you to liaise with Brown for the time being, handle the court side of it. Take down notes, you understand, and bring them to me, not to Brown.'

Blair had been most anxious to emphasise that Jagru was not answerable to Brown and that Brown would have no control over him. As if he understood Jagru's only partially concealed distaste, he had also said that this monitoring job would not last for long.

He wished, almost, that Blair had chosen someone else. But no doubt, in order to get where he wanted, he had to play the lackey's part and act as if he liked it — and if he didn't like it, whom could he tell? Radika and he were drifting further apart. Events at the party had not helped. His mother could be counted on to be sympathetic, but he didn't want to burden her, although he had initially broken down and cried on her shoulder. He would have liked to have talked things over with Asha, but would she have the time to listen and if she did, would she understand?

He picked up Chandi's bag, while his mother sorted out her discharge with the nurse on duty.

Chandi herself seemed much better and appeared to have less worry lines on her face.

He led the way to his car with a little pride. What a beautiful body. It moved so smoothly. The engine almost purred when it went into operation. A vast contrast from the many cars on the road. Whenever he got behind the wheel, he could not help feeling that the whole thing was a dream. He could not be driving such a car. It belonged to someone else. He would soon be back on the road, on foot or running like everyone else to squeeze into one of those ancient, noisy run-down hire vehicles which served the masses.

With very little prompting from Jagru, the car raced through the streets. Within minutes he was at the house he had rented for Chandi and her children. His mother led the way now, ushering Chandi in as if she was presenting a toy to a child.

Chandi moved awkwardly into the new house. The curtains were bright and the furniture gleamed. The images of the shack flitted before her, with its mud floor and its unpainted walls and gloomy interior. She would have gone willingly back to its shelter if she thought she would find her son there. But Das was gone. And her husband? He did not care anymore. He had claimed the whole country with its downtrodden masses as his family and forsaken his own. How did she feel about him now? Before the loss of her unborn child, Das's departure, the pain was raw, giving her frenetic energy to rush about and try and change things, to try to keep a hold on him. She had sought him out, been persistent in her efforts to remind him of his responsibilities. But now she felt a strange remoteness from everything. Wouldn't life still go on even if she was no longer part of it? But she had to rouse herself from this lethargic state. She was a wife, a mother. Lal might not have visited her in hospital, but he would at some point come home. She must ensure that there was food for him, see that his clothes were in order. Had they brought all his things from the shack?

Kunti had gone into the kitchen and now came bustling back with a teapot and teacups and saucers.

Chandi's eyes misted. It seemed like years ago when she had served tea like that with teacups and saucers and a proper teapot. Where had all this crockery come from? She looked the question at Kunti.

'These belonged to my mother,' said Kunti. 'I brought them here on loan until you can get things organised.'

Jagru accepted a cup of tea, protesting weakly, 'I can't stay too long. I've got to get back to the court. They'll be starting the afternoon session in a little while.'

'You've got a fast car,' Kunti said. 'Although I don't like you driving too quickly.'

Listening to them, Chandi smiled. Mother and son seemed so close. Lucky Radika, she thought, to have such a home, where people were so kind. She immediately suppressed the thought as disloyal. Lal had been a good husband. He had done his best for them. They had been happy together until that strange illness of his. And now just because —. She forbade herself the thought. He was her husband for better and for worse.

Jagru put down his cup. The atmosphere was so peaceful, so relaxing. He did not want to get up. 'I've got to go. Can I give you a lift, Ma, if you're leaving now.'

'I'll stay for a while,' smiled Kunti, 'keep Chandi company until her children come.' In a softer voice she added, 'If I'm not there, Radika might pay some attention to little Bunny, instead of leaving him and going out all the time.'

Jagru frowned. Radika. The thought hurt him.

Chandi said: 'I can't thank you enough; you've done so much for me, for my children. So kind to strangers. People you don't know.'

'Thank my mother,' said Jagru. 'She taught me to help others.'

'It was our duty,' Kunti said. 'What a better place the world would be if people helped each other without looking for a return.'

How much better indeed, Chandi thought, as she stood in the doorway, watching Kunti walk out with her son to the car. But things didn't happen like that. Not in reality. You had to pay in some way for every bit of good that happened. This house and the fairy-tale miracle which had given it to her and her children: she would not believe in it. There would be some terrible price she would have to pay. Or had she already paid that price? Was her son, Das, forever lost to her? A cold wind passed over her. Trembling slightly, she retreated into the sitting room. She must stir herself, throw off this passivity which had stolen up on her, go back to her job so that Artie could return to school and she could take some of the burden of the rent off the shoulders of her benevolent friends. She must not allow herself to be fooled into thinking that everything was rosy again or fate was sure to find some new way to punish her.

★ ★ ★ ★

Jagru reached the street where the court building stood. He was in good time. He hesitated for a moment, wondering whether to park his car in a space near the court or somewhere further away. He chose the latter. There were mad people who wandered around the courts and would be quite capable of damaging his shiny new vehicle in some way. He walked slowly down the road, trying to use up the time before the session resumed.

He wondered about a coffee in the shop across the road, but decided against it. He was too well-dressed and did not want to be a target for the embittered loungers outside the shop who might enjoy baiting him.

A girl standing by the court caught his attention. She looked very much like Asha. He chided himself. Was he becoming demented, seeing her in every woman? But then, as he came nearer, he saw that it was Asha.

She greeted him warmly. 'I thought it was you driving that magnificent white car. I was behind in that broken-down old thing.' She pointed to a small red mini nearby. 'I thought you hadn't seen me,' she continued. 'I guess I wouldn't see anyone if I drove a car like that.'

'No, no, it's just that my mind was occupied.'

'Finally got that promotion?' she teased.

Jagru laughed sheepishly as he fell into step beside her. They seemed to be going the same way. Then he remembered.

'So Manu's trial is going ahead?'

'They're probably going to announce the charges today. I promised Manu I would turn up. He had some other business to deal with.'

Jagru forced himself not to ask her if she had progressed any further in her travel plans.

'We seem to be going in the same direction,' Asha observed.

In embarrassment he explained to her his connection with the Additional Court. 'I don't particularly like this business. I mean, I worked with Tyler and some of the others they've charged. I've met them in the course of work. I've been promised, though, that I won't have to do this too long.'

'Perhaps they'll soon move you to another department. Maybe even a notch up the ladder,' she said, 'although you've got to watch your step in that circle. They're a hungry pack.'

Jagru felt pleased at her interest. He was never quite sure what Asha's feelings were about his politics and sometimes wondered whether she might have been more interested in him if he had not got involved in the Secretariat, though at other times he felt sure that she supported what he was trying to achieve, even though she might not necessarily agree with his tactics. He wanted so much for her to be sympathetic. Could he persuade her to have dinner with him?

'I hope everything goes well with Manu.'

'He's very worried. He wants to leave the country as soon as this thing's over. He's just going to pack up everything.'

Jagru's heart lurched. He hated to listen to this talk of leaving. If only he were free. If only he could be sure that she cared even a little for him.

'Can I invite you for a drink after this is over...' he plunged boldly, 'to celebrate my semi-promotion?'

Asha hesitated. She was beginning to worry about Jagru. She sensed the possibility of his entertaining serious feelings for her. She quite liked him, but had no desire for an emotional entanglement. Could she care for him, or anyone? She didn't want to find out. What was she even thinking of? He wasn't available, and even if he was, she feared that she would put too much emotion into a relationship and inevitably fall flat on her face.

'Of course, if you're too busy...' he began diffidently.

'Oh, I'm not busy, not exactly. Let's see later, shall we,' she compromised.

They separated as they arrived in the courtroom. Jagru went to sit at the long table reserved for Counsel. Tyler was sitting with several others on the defendants' bench. Jagru avoided his eyes. He found himself looking at a woman seated at a small table nearby. She was dressed in a most untidy fashion, an unlikely occupant of the press section.

She returned his attention and Jagru felt uncomfortable under the self-possessed stare she turned on him, as if she found him an interesting study. A vague recollection tugged at him. Of course, he mentally snapped his fingers. He knew who she was. What did she call herself now? Ban. He tried but he could not remember her other name. He did not miss the irony of their reversal of roles. He had left his own party to join the Secretariat in the hope that he could accomplish his goals there. She had very publicly left the Secretariat, angrily denouncing it and setting up her own party.

Everyone stood as the magistrate entered the courtroom. Jagru was conscious that he had been noticed. He knew that the magistrate would be affected by his presence, as he was by the presence of members of the press. Their absence at the beginning of the proceedings evidently irritated him and he began the afternoon in a tetchily desultory way.

The cases from the Secretariat seemed to be way down the list. Jagru heard Manu's name being called and a date fixed for the hearing. He looked around quickly. Would Asha leave? But she showed no signs of wanting to do so. As the afternoon droned on, he found it increasingly easy to dissociate himself from his surroundings.

What satisfaction it would be to send Carl Blair to sit in his place, while he sat in Blair's seat of command. Still, he should not complain. How much worse it would be if he were in Tyler's shoes. Poor dog, he thought, like an animal in a cage.

He jumped as the woman orderly suddenly announced in a piercing voice: 'All rise. This court is now adjourned until tomorrow at 09.00 hours.'

They had not called any cases from the Secretariat. How much longer would he have to sit here like this, wasting time?

As he was walking out of the court with Asha, the orderly hurried after him with a piece of paper in her hand. A man who had been dressed in similar clothes to this Jagru Persaud had given it to her, called her out of court to do so.

'Don't disturb him now,' he had said. 'Give it to him when the session is over. But make sure he gets it.'

Constable Smith was sure that both men came from the Secretariat. She didn't think the man who had called her out of court was a minister. She knew their faces; their pictures were always in the newspaper. And this Persaud — he was not a minister yet, but the paper said he was going places. She knew *he* was somebody.

'Sir,' she panted, 'I was told to give you this.'

'Thank you,' Jagru said.

He turned to Asha: 'Shall we go?' They had decided to go to a place called *Diner's Choice*, a genteel establishment.

'Only half an hour, mind,' Asha said, 'then I have to go. Manu will be wanting to know how I got on.'

Jagru nodded. Thirty minutes. Many things could happen in thirty minutes. He felt happy in a stupid kind of way. He told himself not to push it, so they talked of the most commonplace things and he found himself laughing frequently at the slightest provocation. For a moment he felt lifted out of his inadequacies and frustrations. Could Asha make him forget his urge to take on the sufferings of others? Could he go away with her and leave all this behind?

He crushed the thoughts. His sense of release was all too short. She had to go and, as he watched her leave, he only just stifled the impulse to rush after her and beg her to reconsider her decision to leave the country.

He sat motionless at his table, ignoring the anxious glances of the waiter. After a while, he remembered the note the court orderly had pressed into his hand. Mitchell. He had hardly given any thought to Mitchell and the others in his old department since his promotion. He had not even seen Mitchell since the party. Others congratulated him, but Mitchell had not been around when he had gone to clear out his desk. He had not seriously considered Mitchell as one of the prime suspects under investigation, but now he wondered. Certainly, Mitchell had been very jumpy when the investigation was launched. Why did he want to see him and why was he leaving it so late? Ten o'clock. And what an unlikely part of town he had set for the meeting. He would go to meet him, though. He owed him that much. Mitchell had been very helpful, and he was not necessarily in trouble.

But what would he do until ten o'clock? Four hours away. He could go home and spend some time with his son. But that would mean encountering Radika and another of those unprovoked displays of anger. Should he drop in at Manu's? But Asha would surely think him too persistent. He could go back to his new office, but this idea did not appeal, though he had increasingly been using it as a refuge from Radika. Perhaps he could go around by Chandi, see if her husband had turned up and how her daughter was getting on with her new job. His mother might even be there. Yes, that was what he would do.

He was relieved to find his car safe and unblemished. He caressed the door handle for a moment before opening the door. He still could not get over the fact that the car was his.

CHAPTER EIGHT

James Mitchell sat in a darkened corner of the bar, nursing his drink in his hands. From his position, he could see anyone entering. He kept looking at his watch. It was past ten, or was his watch fast? A constant stream of sailors flowed into the bar. From the snatches of conversation he caught, he guessed that a ship had just docked.

'Hey mate,' one of the sailors called boisterously. 'Don't sit there in the dark like that, come over and join us.'

Mitchell shook his head. The dark suited him fine. 'I'll take a rain check,' he called. 'Some other time.' But the sailor's attention had already shifted to the two women who had just come into the bar.

The sailor burst out into a song: 'Good morning Mr Parker, you have such lovely daughters.' He ended to the cheers and jeers of the other sailors and, taking off his cap, swept a deep bow to the two women. 'Evening, ladies, the name is Max. Can I offer you a drink?'

The two women giggled, the light of the bar shining on their painted faces.

Mitchell thought idly how much better they would look if they didn't vaunt themselves so obviously, but perhaps this was part of their charm. At all events, Max the sailor seemed satisfied, and the two women were soon removed from Mitchell's view as they became absorbed into the group.

He resumed his concentration on his glass. Had Jagru got his note? Perhaps the fool would decide not to come. It did not matter to him, one way or the other. He would soon be joining his ship and putting this place and all its backstabbers behind him. But by running away in such a hurry he knew that he would incriminate himself and, if he could, he wanted to put one over on his soon-to-be-former bosses.

Another ten minutes went by. More sailors drifted in. The bar was beginning to look overcrowded and the voices were becoming louder. He thought he could hear angry words from the sailor, Max. He shrugged. Men became heated on 'daroo', the hard stuff, and sailors were notorious for picking fights as soon as they came ashore. *He* would not remain a sailor for long. He had only signed up because it was a convenient way of getting to his eventual destination.

Jagru entered in the middle of the fight which had broken out, took one look and was about to duck out again, when Mitchell's shout reached him. Mitchell ordered his second drink. Jagru wouldn't have anything.

'Thought I would have this little chat with you, before I shake the dust of this place off my feet,' Mitchell said.

'I don't understand.... Are you leaving?' So Mitchell was involved in the investigation in some way. Of what was he guilty?

Mitchell read his thoughts. 'I'm not saying I'm clean, but even if I was I would still get out while the going was good. When certain people make up their minds that they want a few heads for public display, then it's time for people like me, who mind their own business, to start checking their back exits.'

Jagru had become very grave. He understood the sentiment. 'But you've got a contribution to make,' he protested, for form's sake. 'After all, you've got a Ph.D.' He had discovered that Mitchell was considered academically brilliant in some quarters.

Mitchell bared his teeth again. 'You don't think the wolf pack is going to look at pieces of paper with degrees on them, eh?' His tone changed: 'I wanted to talk to you because you seem to be in the middle of this investigation and I don't think you're as naive as some people would like to think.'

Jagru felt that he should resent this statement, but he was becoming interested. What did Mitchell know?

'I think we can scratch each other's backs,' Mitchell continued. 'You know, about some of the things which are going to come out. People say all kinds of things about a man if he's not there to defend himself. I'm not saying that some of the things won't be true, but it's not going to be as bad as they'll make out...'

'I don't quite understand what you're asking me to do,' Jagru said. 'I mean if you feel that Brown or someone else is going to cook things up against you, I don't see how anything I can do will help.'

Mitchell drained his glass. 'Quite, quite, I see your point. I mean nothing they cook up can really stand up in court unless they have papers, documents or the like to support it... Doesn't really bother me, you know. It's my folks I'm thinking about. I'm going to be far away from here in a few hours,' he confided, 'and Rouche, that old bandit, is not going to live forever. Then the rest of the wolf pack will really take over.'

'I'll help, if I can, of course...' Jagru began.

'Don't think that I'm asking your help for nothing, eh. You might find that you *want* to help before all this is over. Some of the people involved might be your friends.'

Jagru stared at him. Manu, he thought, and Asha.

Mitchell laughed. He was beginning to enjoy himself,

freed from the watchful cloak he had donned during office hours. 'Yes, your good friend, Manu and his pretty sister. You've been seeing a lot of her, I understand?'

'They've always been friends,' Jagru protested. 'I'm not involved in their business in any way.' So Manu had been trying to call Mitchell not Tyler as he had assumed. He had thought that it was Tyler's case which drew Asha's attention in the courtroom.

'Oh, I'm not suggesting that you are. But if I were you I would think a little about how *others* know who your friends are and think about who's following your wife around and why the phone makes funny noises.'

This was an inspired guess. He had once seen Jagru and Asha together, but he was pretty familiar with the tactics of the people who moved in Gordon Brown's circles and if Jagru didn't know any better he needed his head examined.

Silence.

Jagru, troubled, considered what Mitchell had said. 'Have you seen the car they've allocated me?'

'Yes, I heard they moved you up. Fattening for the kill, eh? Well, I've done you a good turn by reminding you to watch your back. One good turn deserves another. Think of me on the high seas.'

Mitchell made his way out humming softly to himself. Perhaps he was being an alarmist. He had covered his tracks well. They might never find him out. But it was time to move on anyway. And he had given young Jagru food for thought. The fool. He was whistling as he walked out into the night.

Jagru remained seated, his thoughts whirling, trying to fit Mitchell's words together. He suddenly realised that a woman was leaning over his table.

'Buy me a drink, honey?'

Jagru could smell the sweat that ran down her arms, mixed with a cloying perfume. He found his eyes looking down her dress.

The woman shifted her body suggestively: 'Want to see a good time?' She began to caress his arm.

Jagru pulled his gaze away hurriedly and jumped to his feet. His breathing had become constricted. He made a violent show of pulling his arm away, but then, as he regained his composure, his emotions changed to pity and he turned back to thrust some money into her hand.

'This is for the drink,' he said.

'What's the matter, you an auntieman?' she called after him. She had been joined by another woman and their laughter followed him as he made his way out of the crowd.

But he could not think of them. His thoughts were still on Mitchell. He had always suspected that he was up to something. In a way he was glad that the man would be out of the way. But why had Mitchell sought this meeting? He did not see how he could help, even though he had somehow become inveigled into the investigation. Why were people always assuming that he had more power than he actually had? He thought about Manu and Asha and wondered whether he should go to tell them about his meeting, but dismissed the idea. They were careful people. They would have been cautious. He did not think that they would be easily hurt by their association with Mitchell. But what had he meant by his suggestion about Brown's methods? Was his phone tapped? Well, if they wanted to tap his phone, they were welcome to it. He was not involved in any dubious activities. They were welcome to follow Radika, too. They would no doubt soon find out that they were wasting their time. But it would be interesting to see what happened when they found that Mitchell had skipped. Jagru thought of how

Gordon Brown's face would look. But what exactly had Mitchell been involved in?

The next few weeks shed no light on Mitchell's activities and no hue and cry was raised over his abrupt disappearance. Jagru eventually discovered that he was supposedly on his annual leave. He decided to keep his counsel. He had not come to the Secretariat to become part of any spy ring. However, despite steady hints to Blair when he saw him to present his reports, no move had been made to relieve him of his current duties.

The job was both tedious and uncomfortable. There was that woman Ban who made him feel overdressed, a traitor, if he was honest, to the masses. There was Tyler and the growing number of accused men from the Secretariat and other departments who sat behind him, their hostile eyes boring into his back. There was a tension in the atmosphere, the kind that might induce a man to jump into the box to scream his guilt over crimes about which he knew nothing.

One bright spot remained. Asha was constantly in attendance at the court, even though Manu's case had been fixed for a far-off date. Jagru had originally felt he ought to inform her of Mitchell's flight, but he found a number of reasons for not doing so. After all, he didn't know whether she came to the court because of Mitchell. She had never indicated anything of that nature to him. She probably knew that Mitchell had skipped. What was important was that he was meeting her frequently now. They often had a cup of coffee after the court sessions. An idyllic half hour, the high point of his day.

During one of these coffee sessions, she told him about Manu's abortive attempt to purchase a visa. He had been swindled out of $10,000. Jagru felt honoured to be the recipient of her confidences. He felt that she was becoming more open with him, treating him with greater trust. He tried to talk to her about Radika, without making himself out to be a martyred husband.

'Radika goes her own way these days. I never know what she's doing. She's become so aloof. Sometimes, I think she doesn't live in the house anymore.' He didn't add that Radika seemed to be influencing his daughter against him and that if it wasn't for his mother, he would go home even later than he did. Nor did he tell her that sometimes his mother would not be at home and he would go to find her at Chandi's house, where he was able to relax in an atmosphere so different from his own home.

But he regretted saying anything about Radika. Asha became withdrawn and got up almost immediately, saying that she had to leave, and though she was back again at court the next day, she seemed rather subdued.

Over their coffee, she told him she had been accepted by the overseas college to which she had applied, and that she would be processing her immigration papers shortly.

He did not see Asha again for a long time. She was so busy, getting ready to fly out of his life, he thought gloomily. Surely she must care just a little. He tormented himself with images of her naked, imagining what it would be like to kiss her, to shower her with caresses. He began to think about divorce. Could he actually bring himself to divorce Radika? What would his mother say? Surely she would understand. She would want him to be happy. But Radika, could he desert her? What about those vows they had taken long ago before God and man? Could he let his life be forever knotted up by words he had said when he had no idea of the unhappiness which stretched before him? He could no longer consider Radika. Now he shared only a stranger's bed with her, the tentative overtures of the hungry night firmly rebuffed. There was only Asha.

But his domestic troubles soon gave way in his attentions to events at the Secretariat when Mitchell's departure — *defection* it was soon termed — was discovered.

Jagru was immediately recalled from court, though not returned to his old department. He kept the new office and no-one questioned him about the car. But it was a return to the status quo, in that he seemed to be doing nothing. He did nothing, until the summons came from A.D. James's office.

There were two men with James in his office. They introduced themselves to Jagru, but their names did not mean anything to him. Tom Falder and Harry Rook. Their faces were unsmiling and they did not offer to shake hands. James himself was looking rather grim, by no means the same man who had laughed and joked at Jagru's party.

They wanted to know about Gordon Brown and Blair and other things about which he had not the remotest idea. They kept asking him to repeat the gist of conversations he'd had with Blair. They kept returning to the conversation when Blair had first summoned Jagru to his office.

'Did you have any idea what he meant when he said that he needed a hard core of men in the right place?' Rook asked.

Jagru shook his head. He had not repeated Blair's phrase to anyone. He had even forgotten it. Where had Rook heard it? He remembered Mitchell's hints about the Secretariat's methods. He thought: 'They're investigating the investigators.'

'Why did Blair want you and no-one else to make these reports from the court?' asked Falder.

'Why didn't you make your reports directly to Gordon Brown? After all, he was in charge of the investigation,' Rook fired at him.

Jagru was determined not to allow the questions to intimidate him. He had not been long enough with the Secretariat to behave in the way Mitchell, for instance, might have done.

'I can't answer for Blair,' he said. 'I only did what he asked. I followed instructions.'

'Did you ever chance to hear anything strange while you were in Blair's office?' Rook asked.

James said: 'Perhaps we should tell you that both Blair and Brown are under suspicion for subverting the investigation. We believe them guilty of other things, too.'

'Anything you can remember would help,' said Falder.

Jagru did not know if he had imagined it, but he thought that he saw a signal pass between the men. He wearily maintained that he had nothing to contribute. He had not been in Blair's confidence and knew nothing beyond what the man had instructed him to do.

To his surprise, they did not renew their questioning. After conferring among themselves, Rook and Falder took their leave. James motioned Jagru to remain. 'You've been a great help,' he said.

Jagru was surprised. He had not been conscious of being helpful.

'A great help,' continued James in a more emphatic tone. He added: 'Of course, I don't need to tell *you* that both Brown and Blair are at this moment being placed under arrest.'

Jagru looked at him sharply. What was he up to? He had not forgotten James's performance at his party.

'You will know that we've been preparing the way to make full use of the knowledge and skills you've brought to us. Yes, we've been making ready the right position for you.'

Jagru felt himself go tense: 'What position?' he managed to ask.

James paused. Jagru felt the anger slowly seep through him. Was James stringing him along as they had done before?

'I'm afraid, I'm not authorised to tell you anything as yet. Nothing's been made official, but this sweep's going to take some men out of key positions. However, things go slow here with the PM being so constantly ill.'

Jagru waited. Rouche's illness was a convenient explanation for all sorts of things.

'However, I can tell you we want you to hold Blair's position for a while, until,' he paused for effect, 'the official authorisation comes through.'

Jagru expelled his breath slowly. That made him an executive branch secretary, and Blair had always seemed to operate with far more authority than the title implied. If he read James rightly, he would soon be above that rank. The horizon of his hopes seemed closer than ever. He was back on track, he would confute his enemies. Soon he would be in a position to pursue his goals.

★ ★ ★ ★

'This one's bigger. Cost a dollar more.' Satisfied that she had impressed the additional cost of the plastic bag on the prospective shopper, Aunt Adee began to go through the ritual of unpinning her hoard of plastic bags to get at the one under discussion. This took several minutes, but Aunt Adee, although she noticed her customer's impatience, did not hurry. 'More haste, less speed,' she said.

All around her, the cries of vendors clashed and were sucked into the general incomprehensible babble. Aunt Adee did not add her shouts to the melee. People knew where to find her. A hand tugged at her bags. She turned quickly, thinking it might be a thief or one of those mad roamers. It was a young girl, Chandi's daughter. The eldest one. She looked very smart in her tweed skirt.

'Lord child,' said Aunt Adee, 'you want to frighten the wits out of me!'

'I'm looking for Ma, Aunt Adee. I thought, she might have been here with you. I don't know where she could be.'

'Don't worry child, you ma could take care of sheself real good.'

'She's not been out of the house since she came back from hospital and she hasn't left a note or anything. She just wasn't there when I went home for lunch and I've got to get back to work.' All this came out in an anxious rush.

'She probably gone to look for Lal. You see you father since, child?'

'I don't know what's happened to him. We haven't seen him since Ma went into hospital. Shyam was crying for him last night.'

'Well, ten to one, she gone to look for you father. She a strong woman you ma. You na think she go sit around at home all the time, eh? Don't worry, child. If something wrong she woulda left a note.'

Artie look unconvinced. The burden of her family weighed heavily on her shoulders, especially as she knew that what she earned was insufficient to maintain them and that they were still living on the charity of others.

'Look, that you ma coming over there?' Aunt Adee pointed.

Artie turned eagerly, but the woman was not her mother. Where was Ma? Had she gone to their old place? Her mother was well again. Nothing would be wrong with her. She was worrying unnecessarily. Since she had come out of hospital her mother had looked so much more relaxed. But was this her real state of mind? Artie had the suspicion that her mother occupied some mental state where their problems could not reach her. They had tried hard to prevent anything worrying her — mention of Das and their father was forbidden and Artie had made sure that her mother heard nothing of Janki's offer to leave school and look for a job. But Artie feared that her mother's state of apparent calm could not last. Only last night little Shyam had been crying for his father. Chandi had broken down and cried with her son whilst her daughters watched helplessly. She looked at her watch. She wished there was more time. But what was the use of Ma going to *that* place? He wouldn't be there and they would only take a message. Artie couldn't understand her father, how he could forsake them so totally. She tormented herself, trying to find excuses for him.

'I've got to go, Aunt Adee... If Ma comes, don't tell her I was looking for her. I don't want her to know I was worried.'

Aunt Adee watched her disappear into the crowd. Nice child, she thought. She felt a tear edging its way onto her eyelid. She roughly rubbed it away in horror. She would not remember, and she began to laugh wildly in an effort to block out the image of her only son lying on a cold slab those many years ago.

★ ★ ★ ★

The same woman she had met before was sitting at the desk. Chandi tried to remember her name. The woman looked up, catching her puzzled scrutiny.

'Oh, hello, Mrs Panday,' she said. 'I'm Mitzi. We met before, when you were here about those bullies who photographed you.'

'I would like to see my husband.'

'I'll go see if I can find him for you.' Mitzi got up and moved toward a doorway behind her. 'Won't you please sit?' she said, motioning to a chair.

Chandi remained standing. She would not be lulled by pleasantries.

Another woman came into the room. She had a stack of papers in her hands. Her eyes looked sunken and she walked as if she needed sleep. She smelled strongly of stale sweat. Chandi turned her face away.

'Are you being helped?' she asked.

'I want to see my husband.'

The woman looked at her more fully. 'You're Mrs Panday…' She moved closer to Chandi, stretching out her hand. 'My name's Ban. Your husband is such a great support to us. He's indispensable. I don't think I've ever seen anyone so dedicated.'

'Can I see him?'

'I think he's gone home,' Ban said. 'He was here all night, working …'

'Home,' Chandi echoed stupidly, 'he never comes home. Which place does he call home, now. He's deserted me, his children, all for what? This? This nonsense?'

'Your husband's doing his duty as he sees it. If we could find more like him, this land would become a happy place tomorrow,' Ban said sharply. She turned abruptly on her heels: 'I've got to go. Talk to Mitzi.'

'Where is my husband?' Chandi demanded as Mitzi reentered the office.

'He's just left.'

'Left for where?' Chandi suddenly sat down.

'I think he thought you had gone across the river to live,' Mitzi faltered. She remembered the girl who had brought the message. Somehow, in the rush of things, she'd forgotten to pass it on and then afterwards, she had not known how to.

Chandi stared: 'The river? But how could he possibly believe that? Artie came here. I know she did. Several times to try and meet him.'

Mitzi did not say anything. She averted her face.

'Oh what's the use...' Chandi got up. 'You say he's staying at the old house?'

Mitzi nodded.

Chandi began to laugh. He was at the shack. How funny. Mitzi looked at her in concern. But Chandi's laughing fit had ceased as soon as it had begun. 'I'm going to try and find him,' she said, 'but you'll tell him where we are. You won't try to keep him from his wife and children, eh.'

Mitzi reddened and was about to say something, but Chandi was already on her way out.

Chandi did not know why she had accused them of trying to keep Lal from her. She did not really believe it. The enemy was not these poor deluded people who thought they could change things, the enemy was inside him, eating away at his love for her and the children. Perhaps they *could* change things, but why must it be she and her children who suffered? Why must it be her husband who was sacrificed? Why was he acting as if there was no tomorrow for his family? Tomorrow was another day which had to be met with responsibility.

Chandi soon arrived at the shack. It looked even more miserable than she remembered. Puddles of muddy rainwater surrounding it served as a breeding ground for mosquitoes. Its unpainted boards looked dark and damp, covered in mossy slime. When they had occupied it she had tried to keep the place as clean as possible. Das had gone around picking up dead branches and had spent hours pulling out the weeds which sprang up so quickly after rainfall. 'Das, my son,' she thought, 'my son.' The shack had been a sanctuary of sorts, but a dark and ugly one which had driven her son away and had almost claimed Janki too. She pushed the door open. The hinges creaked. He was lying asleep on a mattress spread out on the ground, breathing in a deep, rattling manner, which sounded as if it hurt. Flies buzzed around the inside of the hut, circling a pile of fruit skins and empty food boxes. Near his hand was a stack of papers. His clothes hung on the lone chair in the room. Chandi could see and smell that they needed washing.

Chandi sat down on the chair, wondering if she could awaken him. He might be angry if he was disturbed from his rest. Why had he not come to look for her? She thought of the house she and her children were now living in, of its comfort. He could not really have believed that she had gone across the river to stay with her father. How could he believe she would have burdened her father in that way?

Lal turned in his sleep and muttered a violent curse. He seemed to have gained a better position, for his breathing had become less laboured and he was snoring in a more normal fashion. Why had he not come? Was it another way of passing on his own obscure pains to her? Chandi tried not to think of the fear which had forced her out of the security and warmth of the house to go and seek him out. Lal could not think that. He could not think that she was a kept woman. He must know that she was a good woman, had always been a good wife, that she would never look at anyone else. She owed a tremendous debt to Jagru and his mother, and one that she had to repay as soon as she could start selling again. Did Lal think that she had found someone else to pay the bills because he was no longer doing it? He could not think that. She had fought so hard to preserve the bonds of their family life, had strained to knot them together again when they seemed to be falling apart.

Lal was groaning in his sleep now. How tired he looked, how gaunt. She would make him come home. She would go out to work again if he was uneasy about living under a roof paid for by another man. How much longer would he sleep? Did she dare disturb him? Artie would be home, wondering where she had gone. Shyam, too, would be arriving home from school. She could not let her children worry. They had cried enough. She would leave and return later. Maybe wait a day or two to see if he would come home. She turned and left the shack.

When she got near the house, she saw someone was sitting on the steps in a hunched position. From the distance, she thought it might be Artie. She hurried, remorseful. She should have left a note. But as she came nearer, she saw the white hairs and realised it was Kunti. Why was she sitting in that manner, hugging her knees as if she was cold?

As Chandi approached, Kunti got up to meet her. Her gait was unsteady and her usually neat hair was in disarray.

'Wicked, wicked,' she muttered, 'wicked woman.'

Chandi, alarmed, stared at her. 'I've done nothing.'

Kunti shook her head. 'Not you. Her. Wicked... Poor Jagru...'

Chandi took her inside, feeling a new energy. The woman's helplessness gave her back a little of her old self, as she quickly assumed command. 'Just relax, while I make you a cup of tea. Then you can talk about it, if you want to,' she added, still a bit unsure of herself.

Kunti sank into the sofa. 'Wicked,' she kept repeating, 'shamefully wicked.' She felt very old and was feeling aches and pains she had not been conscious of before.

* * * *

Radika had pulled the sheet tightly around her. 'Did you think she saw anything?' she asked her companion.

The man did not answer. He was busy putting on his clothes. Paul Bagat had never intended things to go this far. Indeed, he would never have dreamt of going after Jagru's wife had she not almost thrown herself at him on several occasions when they'd met. Somewhere at the back of his mind had been the vague idea of taking revenge on Jagru for his act of betrayal. Jagru had been his guide, his mentor, had taught him to abhor a sick system which placed shackles on the poor, had taught him to understand his goals and to appreciate the distinction between what should be and what was. And then he'd gone across to the enemy, to bed with the organisation which he'd taught him to strive against with all his energy. The act had pierced Paul Bagat to the very core. What did it make him if the man who'd taught him everything he knew was unworthy to have been a teacher? All that he stood for had been mocked. For this Jagru could not go unpunished. He knew that the United Party would not lift a finger; they would accept Jagru's departure with the same resignation they accepted so many things. It was up to him to seek retribution. He had toyed with various ideas and abandoned them. He would bide his time. He had not bargained on Radika.

But now, caught literally with his pants down, by an old woman who could have been his grandmother, all the teachings which were part of his religion came flooding over him. He could still see the shock and horror in the old woman's face, and almost expected to see her still standing in the doorway, immobilised. He cursed himself, feeling like a worm. There was no sweetness in this revenge. He should never have started this. He found that his antipathy toward Jagru had gone, his righteous hatred dissipated and turned sour. There was something else gnawing at his insides. He could not define it, only knew that there was a great dissatisfaction within him.

He tried to smooth the creases in his shirt. He did not look at Radika as she lay languorously on the bed, no longer pursuing the question of what her mother-in-law might have seen. She seemed quite unconcerned about that.

'I've got to go,' he said, finishing the last of his attentions to his clothing. 'See you around.'

'Hey, wait a moment,' Radika said, spurring herself into action. 'What do you mean, see me around?'

Bagat hesitated. He hated scenes, but knew that he could not just walk out on her. 'I think it's best I keep a low profile for a time... the old woman, your mother-in-law. She did see us, you know.'

Radika snapped her fingers. 'I care *that* for her.'

'I still think we shouldn't see each other for a while. We had a good time, but all good things come to an end,' he said, forcing the words out, trying to be brutal. He hoped, though, that she was not going to turn sentimental on him. He hated women who blubbered.

Radika slipped off the bed, the sheet falling to the floor. He stared at her nakedness dispassionately. Her curvaceous body was marred by a thickening around the waist, but she was ripe and sensuous. He remembered how she had grabbed onto him earlier, entwining her legs around him, her suppressed passion exploding in a greedy burst to ignite his own lust. It was a good thing the old woman had not come in when they were locked into each other, oblivious of everything but their driving, grinding compulsion for release. Or had she been there, watching them, mute in her anger, before forcing out that shattering cry of outrage? He tried to shut out this thought.

Radika moved towards him, swaying her hips, aware of the tautness of her body and counting on her ripe nudity to bend him to her will. She moved closer to him, slipping her arms around his neck and rubbing her lips against his cheeks.

'You don't really mean that. You can't really mean you want to leave me. We've had such good times together. It doesn't have to end. I can move out of here if you want me to. You know there's nothing between Jagru and me anymore.' Her hand clutched at his shirt, trying to undo his buttons.

Bagat pulled himself harshly away from her embraces. He felt sated, repulsed. His voice was cold, accusing. 'You said there would be no strings, that it would only be a physical relationship...'

Radika moved away from him to pick up the bedsheet to cover herself. The sheet wrapped around her, she turned to him displaying more sulkiness than anger. 'I'm not asking for more than a physical relationship. You know that very well.'

He felt panicked. What was she trying to force him into?

'I'd rather you didn't leave your husband, really,' he blurted out. 'I've so many things to do. I wouldn't be able to give you the life you want. It's a dull life I live. No fun at all,' he trailed off.

'Well you weren't doing too badly,' she sneered; 'and as for fun, we both know a lot about that, don't we?'

Bagat mopped his brow. Why were some women so bloody-minded? He wished again that he had not started any of this. 'I've got to go.' He tensed himself, waiting for the tirade she would heap on him.

But Radika had become icy, raking him with contemptuous eyes. 'So what are you waiting for, you little wimp? Don't bother coming back!' she called after him, as his footsteps faded down the stairs.

    Radika threw herself on the bed. She was fed up: with the house, with Jagru, with everything. Men, they were so unsatisfactory, so quick to run at the slightest sign of trouble. And why had Kunti come barging into her bedroom like that? What else did they expect her to do? Her son had other women, didn't he? In a way, she was glad that things had been brought to a head. She was well rid of Paul Bagat. Though she'd been beginning to get rather fond of him, he'd shown how profitless that would be. He'd been available and, for a time, a balm to her bruised ego. Perhaps he'd been all the more desirable because he'd been a friend of Jagru and was now his professed enemy. Well, it was at an end. Other things were at an end, too, and others just beginning. Her life with Jagru was over. She would forge a new life in America, join her mother in the land of the free, where no one gave a damn what anyone else did. Perhaps the visas were ready for her and her children. She had applied for them more than a year ago, secretly, after a bitter argument with Jagru who had refused to consider the idea.

    She began to dress. After what had happened today, it would be best to leave the house with her children, find other accommodation until the visas were processed. She would pack just the bare necessities and then she would go and collect little Bunny from the day care centre. Then, if there was still time, she would go around to the embassy.

CHAPTER NINE

'Hot, hot,' muttered Asha to herself, as she wiped her face with a handkerchief almost soaked with perspiration. 'What?' she asked as she became aware that Manu was asking her something.

'Are you sure the forms are filled correctly?' Manu repeated.

Asha looked at the forms again. Of course, she'd filled them correctly. But she did not display any impatience, understanding his anxious state. They were part of a queue of at least two hundred waiting to go into the Embassy. She was appalled and saddened at some of the things she overheard. Money was certainly a good thing to have. True, she and her brothers had worked hard for it — and risked their liberty, but other people worked hard too and risked all kinds of diseases in their unceasing efforts and most of them earned very little. She was glad she had not been forced into to some of the subterfuges she heard about in the conversations around her. She still felt that Manu had been a fool to try and buy a visa. There had been no need and, as she had suspected, the man had turned out to be a swindler, though it was indeed possible to buy visas. There were though many others in the queue who did not share her optimism about being granted a visa, who were more desperate than she had ever imagined.

'We've got to provide for tomorrow,' a stout middle-aged woman wearing a shawl over her head said to her. 'What's there to do in this place? Nothing. My children, they're all very clever. They need a place where they can grow.'

Asha was silent. People felt claustrophobic, as if they couldn't reach out and breathe freely, but what would happen if all the skilled people went? What could one say? How could you tell people not to leave? She was going, wasn't she? But she felt a tremendous pity for the masses who had no choice but to remain and live and die in their deprived state, working to eat and sleep and getting up to face another day. What else was there to do, but leave if you could? Certainly, it made little sense to run about like the half-baked radicals in their vain efforts to oppose the chaos created by the corrupt and inefficient bureaucrats of the Official Party.

The woman next to her had grown silent and was fidgeting as if her feet hurt. The line had grown longer and the midday sun burnt their flesh. It would be another hour before the office opened, but few showed signs of wanting to go for lunch. Many, but not all, had brought food with them.

'I'm hungry,' the woman confided to Asha.

Asha made an embarrassed gesture. Before leaving home she had eaten well. 'I'm afraid I don't have anything I can offer you.'

'Bless you, child, I wasn't expecting you to give me anything. My son's gone off to get a food box at the Carter House,' she said, naming a familiar eating house. She lowered her voice. 'My son, Bub, is very intelligent. We're going to get his papers fixed up. Got married to his cousin, you know.'

'Oh,' Asha said tonelessly. Such confidences were an imposition. She really did not want to know.

A tall, lanky young man ambled up with several boxes in his hands. 'A long line for the food,' he said. 'Was almost afraid I wouldn't be back in time.'

Asha turned away to talk to Manu. She did not care for an introduction to Bub, but Manu, along with some others, was squatting on the pavement, near enough to ensure that their place in the line would not be lost. She found herself worrying, like Manu earlier, about whether the forms were filled correctly. She shook herself mentally. It wouldn't do. It just wouldn't do. She became aware that Bub was trying to get her attention. She made a point of looking in the other direction, but that didn't deter him. He moved closer.

'A very hot day,' he said.

Asha half-turned. Her 'yes' was almost a question, meant to daunt. But Bub seemed to find encouragement.

'Yes, a real hot day. So you trying to get out, too.'

Asha was repelled. He sounded so crude. 'I'm trying to get a visa, yes,' she said coolly.

Bub did not seem to notice her tone. 'I'm getting out soon. Through my cousin, you know. We got married. Not a real marriage,' he added somewhat hastily, 'she just helping out the family. That's how we do it. Help each other out.'

Asha muttered something inaudible. Bub seemed to find further encouragement in her silence.

'I'm looking for a nice girl, you know, to marry eventually.' He pressed on, 'Can you cook?'

'I never cook,' she said somewhat tartly.

'Oh,' Bub said. But he was not put out for long. 'What do you do in the evenings? We live in the country, but sometimes, I come up to town. I like to spend a little time here. I'm not due to leave here for another month or so.'

Asha was saved from answering by the sudden rush

towards the gates. The line, which had been so assiduously held, disintegrated. But it soon assumed shape again, as the official behind the gate indicated the need for order. He began to collect passports and official forms, but allowed only ten people at a time to pass through the gates.

Asha began to regain her confidence, although Manu looked pale. 'Don't worry,' she whispered. They had proven financial resources and they would not be subjected to any great bureaucratic delay. But was there really any difference between herself and Bub? They were all beggars at the gate.

★ ★ ★ ★

Jagru drove through the city, the smooth purring of the car engine responding to his exhilaration. It had happened at last. In comparison to this, the discovery that Radika had fled from their home paled into insignificance. He thought briefly of her embittered face, of how she had ordered him from the flat to which she had taken the children. He had gone to discover what the separation meant and to reassure the children of his love, though mostly because he knew his mother would have wanted him to go. But Kunti had been strangely silent, lost in her thoughts, making no response when he had talked about Radika's departure. But it was not to his mother that he was carrying his triumph. She would be happy for him, happy that it had happened at last, but he would see her in good time. It was to Asha he was bearing his prize. He exulted in the thought that he could now try to win her in earnest, now that Radika had taken off. Things were finally happening his way. First that tremendous step forward at the Secretariat, and then maybe, who knew? Yes, his star was high. The decisions he had made had not been foolish. The thought of really having something to tell her made him feel energetic, in a way he had not done for a long time. He felt like laughing out loudly, almost crazy in a delirium of joy.

The car suddenly shot forward with a great lunge as if his body had communicated its excitement to the accelerator. He tried to control himself, to become the sober, old Jagru, but he felt like a young boy who had gained something he really coveted. He laughed out aloud. Yes, these things he *had* coveted.

He bounded out of the car, hoping she would be there, waiting. He found pleasure in the thought of her waiting for him. As his eyes got used to the darkened interior of the cafe, he made out the familiar features. Yes, she was indeed there, waiting.

A glow of contentment spread over him. She had come early, that signified much. Should he have brought her some flowers? But perhaps, that would have been too gauche. He still did not know her very well, could not really interpret her moods. That would come. He was carefree, boyish as he tiptoed up behind her, trying to startle her. But she turned around before he could touch her, a smile forcing its way on her lips as she saw how she had spoiled his surprise.

'I heard,' she said, greeting him. 'It was on the radio.'

He felt momentarily cheated, but his mood was too buoyant to be spoiled. 'I didn't know it would be on so soon. I wanted to tell you immediately. I felt you would understand what it meant.'

She laughed. 'You think so?'

'Champagne to celebrate?' This hour was his. He would forget all other considerations. 'You know, Asha,' he said, 'it's not so much the prestige of being a minister, as the things one can do, the good things... Although I suppose some would see it differently. They would say it's a disgrace for anyone to be a minister under this system.'

'I suppose in the end, it's what you do that matters, not what others think,' Asha said.

Jagru grabbed at her words. 'I was sure you'd understand. I was sure you'd see that I wasn't just currying favour with the people at the top for the sake of getting perks, although, if you're in Rome, you've got to act like the Romans.'

Asha had fallen silent. She seemed to be caught up in her own thoughts.

'But I'm boring you,' he cried.

'No, no,' she protested. She smiled brightly at him as if to support her words. She wasn't sure if she wanted to be sitting here listening to Jagru. She'd managed to keep apart, to remain as a distant observer, looking on at this panorama of bad times. But Jagru's energy made her wonder if she shouldn't abandon that role, become more active. Perhaps change was possible, if people joined together in hope and determination. She shook her head. She would not allow herself to be drawn into a senseless battle, she would not let Jagru mesmerise her.

'They didn't say which ministry you'd be heading...'

Jagru looked almost boyish. 'Actually, I haven't been given a single ministry as such. I'm Minister in the Ministry of Planning. Preferable,' he added quickly, 'to being minister of any other department.' He was going to enlarge on his plans, but stopped himself, though he was bursting with ideas. He wished his former colleagues could see him now. They would understand what had led him to move across, understand that he would make a difference. But here was Asha sitting in front of him. She did not know yet that Radika had cleared out. He tried to think of a way to tell her without making it seem too much like happy news.

The waiter placed the champagne bottle before him.

'Just a little,' Asha said, her face clouding.

He popped the cork. Didn't she like champagne? He rarely drank alcohol, but this was an occasion, a double one, and no ginger ale would suffice.

'To our dreams,' he said, raising his glass.

'To your dreams,' Asha responded.

Jagru drained the glass. Could he screw up sufficient courage? Dutch courage, he thought. He put his glass down, leaving his hands free. Asha looked straight ahead. She kept wetting her lips. He reached across the table to grasp her hand, feeling as intense an emotion as he had felt earlier, when A.D. James had informed him of his ministerial role and showed him the authorisation which came from PM Rouche.

'Asha,' he began. He felt her stiffen and relaxed his hold. 'Asha,' he began again, 'so many things I want to tell you... and I don't know how to say any of them.'

'I'm leaving, Jagru,' Asha said, keeping her voice steady, 'in a few days. My ticket is already purchased. In my purse,' she gestured.

Jagru did not look at the purse. He would not allow a purse to defeat him, not on a day like this. He began to caress her hand.

'Radika has left. She packed up and went yesterday. I think she wants a divorce.' He continued to caress her hand.

Asha felt she should pull her hand away, but did not stir. She watched fascinated, his fingers playing on her hand. 'I've got to go,' she said helplessly. 'You knew I meant to leave, that I always planned to go overseas. I've got my studies.'

'Asha,' Jagru said caressingly, in command of the moment, 'you know how I feel about you, don't you. You know how much you mean. You're so intelligent, so wonderful, so beautiful. Think of the things we could do together. I know you care about people, about things in the same way I do. Think of the things we could achieve.'

Asha tried to dispel the effect of his words. She knew what she had to say. 'I'm sorry, Jagru. I'm really sorry.'

'You don't mean that, Asha. I know you don't. Before it was different. I had commitments. I couldn't even attempt to win your affection. But now, now I want to tell you how much I love you. I want to tell you not to stop yourself liking me, even just a little. Just a little. That's all I'm asking for now. Don't go away where I can't see you. Give me time. Just a little time to convince you how much you matter.' Jagru was surprised at his eloquence; the words seemed to flow. He could not let her leave. He had to make her understand how important she was to him. He had to.

Asha was shaking her head. Really, this was serving no purpose. The sensible thing would be to get up and leave, not to prolong the discussion any longer. But she did not move. She could not quite bring herself to get up and walk away.

'All my travel arrangements are already made...'

It was Jagru's turn to shake his head. 'Travel arrangements can be changed.' Silence greeted this remark. Jagru felt worn out by his eloquent outburst, although his confidence was by no means shattered. Perhaps, he was going about this in the wrong way. He was pressing too much.

'How soon do you plan to leave?' he asked, gently.

In a few days? Panic overwhelmed him. Could she really mean to go out of his life forever? In a few days? What could he do?

'So I won't see you again after today?'

'I think I'm going to be too busy.' Asha tried not to look at him.

He reached out for her hand again. 'At least spend a few more hours with me. If only I could make you change your mind...' Did she really not care for him? Why had she agreed to meet him, then?

Asha moved her shoulders in a helpless fashion.

'A few hours?'

She attempted a laugh. 'It's a gloomy place to spend a few hours. We can't drink champagne all the time.'

Jagru saw his chance. But she would not want to come to his house. What was he thinking of? He could not take her there.

'I know somewhere we can go,' he said, waiting for her objection.

Asha did not say anything. She toyed with the napkin on the table. He felt a renewal of hope. Perhaps he could still persuade her. He turned to attract the attention of the waiter.

'Shall we go?'

★ ★ ★ ★

She had come out without a hat or a shawl. The piercing midday sun blazed down on her, making her head ache, but she ignored the effects of the sun as she laboured down the street. Kunti knew where she was going. She had been there before, on the rare occasions she had visited Jagru at his old workplace. But after he left, she had not imagined there would be any reason to set foot in the place again — not that she disliked any of the people, although she suspected that they had been less than kind to Jagru on his departure. She was angry that she had to make the journey, but she had to go now, and see that brazen young man, even though she would have liked a good long rest instead. She would tell him that he had no right to go running around violating other people's homes, that he should be ashamed, but when she approached the building, her steps faltered.

She tried to imagine the words she would say. But was he the right person to say them to? Perhaps she should have gone to see Radika instead. Could she entrust that woman with her grandchildren? Wicked, wicked, she thought. The sun made her head hurt, but rest in front of the building revived her somewhat. She climbed the stairs. He was the first person she saw as she arrived at the top. He was shameless to sit there like that, all innocence, as if he had not been parading about in her son's home, a little while ago, naked, bent on his evil deeds. What kind of generation was it that knew nothing of right and wrong?

Paul Bagat gaped at the old woman, remembering all too precisely the circumstances in which they had last met.

Kunti shook her fist at him. 'You, you...' But her tongue had suddenly gone dry. The room began to go around. She saw a man coming towards her, his hand outstretched.

His hair was white and he had a vague resemblance to someone she had once known. It was her husband. It had to be him, though he had never been that old, his face so creased with lines. But her last conscious thought was that the brazen young man, that fiendish devil, seemed to be standing upside down.

★   ★   ★   ★

Asha followed Jagru as if in a daze. She saw him push his hand in his pocket and pull out a crumpled note which he pressed into the hand of the man at the desk. She could not see the denomination and occupied herself by wondering what it might have been. She did not want to think about why they had come to this place or why the man at the desk leered at her in such a filthy manner.

The man was fumbling in a drawer now. He brought out a single key which he handed to Jagru in what was meant to pass as a surreptitious manner. He sank back into his chair and raised a tattered magazine, as if to hide his presence behind it, but as he pushed his eyes above it to peep at Asha, the magazine slipped from his hand and Asha saw that his teeth were rotten.

What was she doing here? What was this place? But it was obvious what this place was. She could not fool herself to think otherwise. She should not be going with him in such a passive manner. She should turn and leave. But her legs did not obey her. She found herself following him through the long corridor, cringing aside to let a woman in a flimsy nightdress go by.

Jagru fumbled with the lock, but the key turned easily. He stood aside, holding the door for her to enter. His eyes shone with excitement, oblivious of her mood.

Asha walked into the room slowly. The mixture of stale human smells assailed her nose. The room was dark, almost musty. She could not take her eyes off the bed in the corner, with its old faded sheets. What spell was Jagru weaving on her? She did not really care for him in this way. She should not be here with him. She ought not to be here.

Jagru had taken her hand. The condition of the room did not seem to affect him. He was intent on her, a triumphant expression on his face. 'Beautiful Asha,' he whispered, as he led her towards the bed. She sat stiffly on the edge, as if this posture would dissociate herself from the room. He placed his arms around her, tentatively kissing her lips. His hands moved towards her blouse, playing with the buttons, clumsily trying to undo them.

Asha stared at him as if she were a petrified rabbit caught

in a trap, as he slowly pressed her down onto the bed, his body moving to cover hers, with a practised skill she had not suspected in him.

The mustiness of the room suddenly overwhelmed her.

'I need air,' she gasped. Lost in his exploration of her body, Jagru did not take in her words.

His enjoyment was exquisite, his being pulsating, the sound of loud drums pounding madly in his ears. The ultimate ecstasy — that Asha would finally be his, body and soul.

'I need air!' Asha cried, her voice louder in renewed urgency. Jagru at last became aware that she was struggling, trying to get him off her. He sat up in concern. Had he hurt her?

Asha got up from the bed, rearranging her clothes. She studiously avoided his eyes, as she dusted herself with a vehemence which found its echo in rising clouds of dust in the room.

'Asha...' Jagru began, realising that she was upset.

She turned to him finally, her voice cold with anger. 'Look at this place. Just look at it. How could you bring me here. How could you presume? How could you?'

Jagru looked, seeing the squalor for the first time. In his desire to win Asha, he had shut his eyes to everything else. Now as he looked at the dusty, squalid room, he realised that he had made an immense mistake in trusting to the judgment of the colleague who had given him the address of the place. He should have known better. He turned helpless eyes towards Asha, begging her to understand.

She ignored his mute appeal. 'I really can't stay here,' she said, still coughing. 'I don't think any of this has been a good idea.'

Jagru tried to protest, but no words came. His energy had

disappeared, his body had gone limp. He could not have made love to Asha now, even if she were willing.

She had stopped coughing. She stretched out her hand. 'I'm sorry,' she said, 'I guess this is goodbye.'

He got up, drained of protest. 'I'll come with you, walk you out of here.'

'No, no,' she exclaimed in horror, picturing new scenes where he devised new ways to keep her by his side.

He seemed to see her in slow motion. She was going, forever, and there was nothing he could do. Nothing, except prolong the agony. He had bungled it.

'Asha I didn't mean to hurt you. I wouldn't hurt you for the world. All this,' he waved his hand at the room and the bed, 'I wasn't thinking straight. I don't know what got into me.' His voice was dull, lifeless.

'Never mind, Jagru.' She was composed, almost relieved now that she had found a way out of the situation. 'It's all right. I do understand. And please don't come with me. I can find my way out.'

'But…' He did not say anymore. He sat down on the bed.

Asha hesitated by the door, then quickly moved towards him, for a moment moved by his dejection. She placed a fleeting kiss on his brow, then glided away before he could realise what had happened. 'It wouldn't have worked out,' she said as she regained a strategic position near the door.

He did not respond. The clicking of the door grated and he buried his head in his hands to dull the drumming sound of her heels moving away down the corridor.

A knock on the door roused him from his stupor. He did not move immediately and found that the door was being opened from the outside. It was the man from the desk. He had a bunch of keys in his hand.

'So you all right,' he said to Jagru. He winked. 'What

happen? Me see you piece walk outa here. A real knockout. Things na work out?' He licked his lips, confident that the details would be worth elaborating on later as a story for his woman.

Jagru remained silent, defeated, on the bed. The man stared at him sullenly, gauging his silence. Never mind, he could always invent the details.

'You time's up,' he said. 'If you want you can pay for another hour. Though me don' know what you gon do with an hour in here. You could play with youself, I suppose,' he sneered.

Jagru got up. He looked around the room. He could have sat there, finding a bitter release in its dinginess, but perhaps a bit of fresh air would do him good.

'I'm leaving,' he said, brushing past the man.

'What about my bloody tip?' the man shouted after him. 'Who do you think's going to make up this bed, clear up you filth? You go want to come again, you know.'

Jagru did not reply. This was the last thing he could imagine wanting.

Bright sunlight, too bright, flooded his face as he stepped out into the open. He began to walk back towards the cafe where he'd had lunch with Asha. His car was still parked there. He pictured her sitting at the table, laughing with him. How long ago had it been? An hour? Two hours? It seemed like an eternity ago that he'd actually held her in his arms and dreamt of spending a lifetime with her.

He got into his car and drove aimlessly, slowly, with no real place to go. He could not go back to his office for indeed he had as yet no office and had won a free day while the Secretariat organised the vacating of an office for him. After a while, he thought of his mother. She would be wondering what had become of him. His mother would be glad for him, but he did not know if he could go through the motions of being happy. But he turned the car towards his home, making an effort to pull himself together.

As he turned into the driveway, he could see that someone was at his door. He saw with a shock that it was his former colleague and friend, Paul Bagat. As he emerged from the car, Paul hurried down the stairs to greet him.

'I heard the news. Congratulations,' he said, not offering to shake hands. Bagat shifted his eyes about on Jagru's face, eventually focusing his gaze on a spot beyond him.

'What can I do for you?' Jagru asked, trying to make himself sound friendly. He had nothing against Paul, who had been his friend for many years. Maybe, now that he was Minister, they might even be able to work towards some official level of understanding between their parties, if nothing else. There were several in the old party who had brilliant minds. Their contributions could be significant if they were allowed to make them.

Bagat was hesitant, uncomfortable. Jagru could see that he was struggling for words.

'Anything wrong?'

'Your mother.' Bagat faltered, wincing as Jagru gripped his arm.

'What about my mother?' He released Bagat's arm suddenly and made an abrupt dash for the stairs. He was almost halfway before he pivoted in shock as Bagat's next words reached him.

'She's in hospital.'

He ran down the stairs to stand before Bagat who blurted out a story that made little sense to him. The whole thing sounded insane. What had his mother been doing at his old party's offices? It seemed a most unlikely place for her to visit.

'She fell down before she could say what she had come for. I think the heat was too much for her,' Bagat volunteered, as if Jagru had accused him.

Jagru wasn't really listening. He could think only of his mother lying on some hospital bed. He could not remember a time when he had not had his mother, could not ever remember her not being there.

He drove quickly towards the hospital and spent a frantic half hour trying to discover where she was being treated. When he did discover where she was, the woman in charge of the ward would not let him in.

He pleaded with her. But she said that she was just an employee, following instructions. Then he remembered that he was a minister, a minister of state and that he was in a state institution. His voice became cold, hard, as he informed the woman of his status, though inside he was still a quivering mass of terror and apprehension.

The nurse's attitude underwent an immediate change. Respectfully, she informed him that someone would escort him to the patient.

'Nurse Jacob,' she called. The woman who came had a reassuring smile, which Jagru wanted to believe in.

He scanned the beds. Where was his mother and what was wrong with her?

Once they were out of earshot, Nurse Jacob said: 'You mustn't take any notice of that old battleaxe. She has her good days, but they're very few.'

Jagru did not seem to have heard. 'Nurse,' he gulped, swallowing his spit, 'what's wrong with my mother?'

She looked up in surprise at the question. 'Mrs Persaud. Kunti Persaud?' She did not wait for the confirmation, but continued cheerfully, 'They reckon she was just weak and the heat got to her. Needed some blood. But nothing to worry about. She's already recovering. We'll soon have her out of here.'

But Jagru had stopped listening to her. His mother was lying on the bed. She looked still, almost lifeless. All his fears returned. He moved closer. He saw that she was breathing and that her features were not as pallid as they had appeared from a distance. He picked up her hand. She stirred slightly but did not awaken. Nurse Jacob left him but within minutes was back with a chair. He took it gratefully.

Would she be all right? He held on to his mother's hands. They were cold. Why were they so cold? He wished he could demand answers from someone, but Nurse Jacob had discreetly moved away. Tears gathered around his eyelids. Ma had always been there for all the crucial moments, to share his happiness and his sorrow. When, on his marriage, she would have left to seek other quarters, it was he who had insisted that she remain. She had sacrificed too many of her good years to make him what he was. She should have been there today to share his momentous news, instead of lying in the hospital like a pale shadow. And he had rushed to Asha with his news about the ministerial post. He would get them to put her in a private room. He could well afford it.

He hurried to the desk to execute the task. The battleaxe was coy about his request. She assured him that they would move his mother to a private room as soon as the doctor came. She feigned ignorance about the cost. It was, of course, a state hospital, but she mentioned almost diffidently that if he wanted a nurse on a private basis, that would, of course, be extra.

His burst of energy satisfied, Jagru returned to his mother's bedside. Kunti was still sleeping and indeed looked peaceful. He sat for a while looking at her, reluctant to disturb her rest. He would leave and return later. He had a word with the duty nurse to indicate his willingness to pay for extra attention and to stress that he wanted a word with the doctor as soon as possible.

'I can't say when the doctor will be in,' the nurse told him. 'But,' she consulted her chart, 'the evening doctor will be here in another three hours.' She summoned up a smile. 'She's going to be all right.'

Jagru thanked her, feeling a rush of gratitude for her attempt at being pleasant, although he suspected that it had been prompted more by knowledge of his ministerial status than respect for his emotions as a human being.

For a moment he felt comforted, but as he drove away, a full sense of his desolation returned. As his thoughts switched between Asha and his mother, his depression grew heavy on his shoulders. He had never had greater need of his mother, whose presence would have been a solace to his wounds, who had always been there in his hour of need. Who could he turn to now? He had a desperate desire to unburden himself to someone who would be understanding and sympathetic.

★ ★ ★ ★

Chandi found herself laughing foolishly. She laughed and kept laughing in a way which had been alien to her in recent times. Tears streamed down her face as she continued to laugh. Flushed with happiness and wearing the new print dress which dear, dutiful Artie had bought for her the previous day, Chandi was looking something like the woman she had once been. She read the letter once more, but before she had finished, she was laughing again. She held the edges of her dress and twirled around in a little dance and then almost skipped towards the sofa.

The letter was from her son, her dear son, Das. He was working with a cruise line. He had left the smugglers almost immediately after he had joined them, working at several jobs before landing this one. The letter, which by a miracle, she felt, had found its way to their new address, was full of apologies, remorse and a money order. The latter Chandi paid little attention to; it was his news which gave her an overwhelming peace. Das was all right. He would be all right. He had chosen to work. She would have much preferred him at home, getting along with his studies, but she was glad that his job appeared to be one which would keep him out of trouble. It was enough to know that he was safe and well. She began to sing a long forgotten tune.

★ ★ ★ ★

Lal Panday pressed his fingers to his forehead, trying to still the dull ache which pounded there. He was tired but refused to give in to the limitations of his body. He heaved himself out of his chair having completed the speech he was writing, a denunciation of the so-called 'clean-up campaign'. He had earlier done a piece for the party's news sheet on the Third World debt problem, in which he had attacked not only the role of the IMF, but the greedy tinpot Caesars of the Third World, whose pockets had a never ending capacity for the people's money.

Lal would not admit that he was weary. A fierce energy burnt within him, fuelled by the same anger which had made him capable of forsaking his own in order to fight for what he felt was a greater cause, to fight for a better tomorrow for everyone.

But now, his speech finished, he frowned, the existence of his family once more intruding on his thoughts.

'You won't forget to go and see them. She was most anxious, your wife,' Mitzi had urged, as she brought him a steaming cup of coffee. He supposed he ought to go and see them. He had been glad to think that Chandi and the children had gone across the river to stay with her father. He had needed to forget his obligations to them, if he was to devote his very being to the struggle. But the journey was a long and weary one. It sucked at his strength. He could not admit the possibility that his cause was like a whirlpool that might suck him down as a spent force into its vortex.

He got up. He would go and try to find this place where they lived. Although he hardly thought about it, he was aware that the shack was not exactly healthy. It would be good to get out, no doubt. But how were they living in such a good area and who was paying for it? It could not be the old man. He knew that Chandi's father had no great wealth. He pursued this line of thought, finding in it only cause for disquiet.

★ ★ ★ ★

Jagru had no idea that he was going to visit Chandi until his car turned into the street where she now lived. But as soon as he realised where he was heading, he found the idea welcome. Chandi had such a soothing presence. She would understand.

He did not know how much he would tell, but certainly she would grasp what his mother's illness meant to him. An insidious thought crept into his mind that if he had appreciated Chandi's quite different attractions all those years ago, instead of Radika's smiles and wiles, how different his life might have been. If Radika had not forced that great emptiness on him, would he have chased after Asha?

But he banished these thoughts as images of his last meeting with Asha turned like a knife in the wound of his mind.

Chandi welcomed him with some pleasure, bursting to tell her own news and he had to sit down and listen to an account of her son's adventures before he could impart his own gloomy tidings about his mother. She listened in grave silence, her demeanour soothing him and encouraging his outpourings.

His mother had always been well, he had never known her to be ill. Chandi nodded. She would not let on that she knew more, reveal Kunti's confidences when they had met recently. What Jagru's wife did was her business, but she could not show surprise when Jagru told her that Radika had left the house. Jagru fell silent after he had spoken of Radika's departure. He had not intended to talk about her, but Chandi's little nods had served to encourage him. He really wanted to talk about Asha, to pour all his frustrations about her into sympathetic ears, but he did not see how he could do so now.

He moved back to the safer territory of his mother's illness. He hoped she was going to be all right, that she would recover quickly and get back on her feet again. He had seen her, but they had given her a sedative, so he had not been able to talk to her.

Chandi nodded. 'I'm sure she's going to be all right. Your mother is a strong woman and a very kind one.'

Jagru felt convulsed with emotion. Her sympathy was so healing. He found that his shoulders were heaving and discovered to his alarm that he was about to lose control of his emotions. He felt Chandi's arm pressing him on the shoulder. He tried to salvage his self-control. He clutched at Chandi in the effort and found that in holding her in a rough embrace there was a sweet release from his pain.

Chandi felt her body go rigid as Jagru grasped her, but she did not pull away. She was a mother. A mother of five. He could not see her other than as a mother and if he found a few moments of comfort by clinging to her as a child would, why should she object? He had done so much for her.

She did not know when she realised that his mood had changed and he was no longer clinging to her like a child. But she did not pull away as all her instincts cried out that she should. She was so indebted to him. Instead she withdrew into herself, distancing her thoughts from the feel of his hands.

It was Jagru who pulled himself away first, abruptly, shocked at himself. 'I'm sorry,' he said, his face pinched.

In the same moment they both became aware of the figure by the door. Chandi jumped up, her face drained of all colour.

'Lal,' she cried, then stood there in confused embarrassment, restraining herself from the eager greeting which pressed for expression.

'Lal, indeed,' the man repeated mockingly. Chandi flushed and bit her lip.

'It's not what you think...' Jagru began, wishing that his display of weakness had never been or that it had not been witnessed by this wild-looking, malnourished man. This must be Lal Panday. He had not at first realised that Chandi's husband and the Worker's Party militant were the same person, but seeing him now he recognised him from newspaper photographs.

The recognition seemed mutual. 'I don't believe you're privy to my thoughts, Mr. Minister,' Panday jeered. 'And further more, whatever rights you may have here, don't you think that it would be the decent thing for you to clear out while I'm here. We poor politicals who have to live on bread and water can't afford the fancy tastes of ministers, you know, who can keep their mistresses in a better condition than we can keep our wives. But we still have some rights.'

Jagru clenched his fists and unclenched them. Such vile insinuations. He felt like lashing out, but remembered himself in time. Panday would love to have such a scene. He shuddered. The headlines in the straggling news sheet which Panday's party produced would be unpalatable to say the least. He looked at Chandi who stood there appalled.

'Aren't you going to leave?' Lal Panday repeated. Jagru realised it was best not to prolong the scene. He could only cause further harm by defending himself and Chandi. He had already, unthinkingly, caused Chandi much grief. He stumbled towards the door and began to walk clumsily down the stairs.

As the sounds of his footsteps died away, Chandi said quietly, 'He was telling the truth, Lal.'

The words seemed to infuriate him further. 'Truth,' he thundered, 'Truth. You think I don't know about those jackasses from the Secretariat. Nothing would make me believe that there's a spark of decency in any of them. Sell their own mother's if they could.'

'You don't know Jagru,' said Chandi. 'He and his mother were so kind, they helped the children so much when I was in hospital, found this house for us, a job for Artie...' her voice trailed off. She remembered her own conviction that nothing was ever gained for nothing. Was Lal's disbelief the price she would have to pay for the benevolence of strangers.

'Why should I know Jagru?' he sneered. 'You know him well enough for both of us, eh?'

She cried out in pain as he gripped her arm.

'So you had to find someone else. You couldn't keep, Chandi, not when the hard times came. What would you have done if I'd been crippled?'

But you weren't crippled, she wanted to shout at him, and I didn't find someone else. But she kept silent, not wanting to enrage him further.

Her silence seemed to goad him and he made a savage attempt to rip off her dress. The new material resisted his efforts. They were lying on the floor now and Chandi cringed as he forced himself upon her, savagely pushing her legs apart. Needles of pain shot through her, reminding her that it had not been very long since she had lost her child.

He misunderstood her aversion and with calculated brutality set about to master her body.

Chandi lost touch with herself. She thought she could see a tranquil calm sea somewhere and she in a little boat, sailing away into the horizon. She became aware that the hacking away at her body had ceased. Her husband was sitting next to her, his body wracked by sobs. She herself felt nothing. Both her body and mind were numb.

She did not know whether or not she was angry with him. She saw the ragged, driven man who had almost become a stranger to her, who had brutally imposed his will and body on her, but she saw too the young man with bright eyes, speaking eagerly of the things he meant to do, of the future he would build with her. She felt disgust and an immense pity for both of them. Awkwardly, she got up from the floor. She could not bear to listen to his sobbing and between anger and pity went to sit next to him. They sat together for a long moment, the bitterness and anger which he had forced into the atmosphere dissipating in the silence. He placed his hands around her tenderly. Chandi did not resist his embrace. She was a good woman, had always been a good woman. How could he have thought otherwise? She did not put the thought into words. She would not spoil this moment of rare peace — and Lal looked so shattered, as astonished as she was that he had given way to this unfamiliar rage.

He took Chandi's face in his hands. 'Chandi,' he said, 'these times are hard times and I know how hard they are, especially for you. I wanted to live a simple life, to be a simple man, one of the thousands who just want to get on with their lives in any way they can, to welcome tomorrow as another day where they can provide in peace for their families. But how long can a man endure when all dignity's lost. Nothing's wrong with hard work when you're providing for your family, but everything's wrong with passively accepting a system where your money can't buy food for your children, where...' he checked the long speech he was about to embark on. 'All I wanted to say, Chandi, is that someone had to do it and it turned out to be me. I know that I've caused you pain and suffering. I hope you'll understand that what I'm doing has to be done. Has to be.'

Chandi understood his sincerity, but she would never understand how a man could forsake his own. She couldn't let them starve when tomorrow came. How could he? But she said nothing. He had made his decision long ago. Nothing she could say would influence him now.

Even in his remorse, she doubted that he believed her innocent of bartering her body to Jagru in order to pay the bills, though, after his assault, he seemed to think that the matter deserved no further attention.

Could she forgive him? Did he think his tears washed away the incident, purging him of his guilt?

His vulnerability made him seem like another of her flock wanting reassurance. She wiped her eyes. It was enough that Lal was back. Beyond that she would not question. She would not open the Pandora's box of her feelings to think about the violence he had forced on her body, nor about his baseless suspicion against her. She did not have that luxury.

She would return to work at the market. Perhaps they would soon be able to pay the rent that way. She remembered the money order which had come with the letter. There had to be some way to provide for her children so that they would not have to toil before it was their time to do so.

She followed her husband as he moved towards the bedroom. He dropped onto the bed and was immediately asleep. Chandi watched him for a while, knowing that he would sleep for some time and that soon little Shyam would be home and overjoyed to see his father. Why couldn't they have stayed a simple family, as he had said, playing out their lives as so many ordinary people did, living each day as it came? If the country was in chaos, what business was it of a simple family man who had to provide for his own? The question made her head ache. She went in search of painkiller to ease the throbbing.

CHAPTER TEN

He was running, running as fast as he could. But they were gaining on him. Their searchlights ripped apart the protection of the night. He made one last spurt, but someone had him in the sights of their rifle and even before he succumbed to the tangled vines which caught his feet, the silence of the night was being disturbed and the redness of his blood staining the back of his shirt.

Aunt Adee twisted and turned, straining as the nightmare came to its inevitable conclusion. Her son had been dead many years now. She had not been a witness to his death, but her nightmare seemed to know all about it, fed by the scraps of information given her by the authorities when they handed over his body. He had been shot while escaping arrest. But her son had always been a good boy and, if they had found him doing something he shouldn't have been doing, they should have given him a fair chance and not made him another of the many 'escaping arrest' victims.

Aunt Adee was sitting up now, the horror of the nightmare slowly losing its grip. From her position in one of the stalls outside the market, she peeked out at the sky, its crimson splashes heralding the dawn of another day. As the light came up from the east, the shadows of her dream were banished along with the receding darkness. She had not dreamt of her son for a long time, could not remember when she had dreamt him so vividly, except when they had carried her to that place where they treated people for nervous breakdowns. She wondered hesitantly whether she should search the dream for a hidden meaning, then felt there couldn't be any. She did not want to remember her son more than she already did.

A cold wind began to blow, but Aunt Adee did not feel the chill. She was insulated from the cold by the plastic bags pinned around her body. People were beginning to pass the stall, the seven o'clock workers. The shop across the road would soon be open and she would be able to get her morning cup of tea. But as she eased herself down from the stall, she had a better idea. She would go now, while the day was still young, to visit her friend Kunti, instead of in the afternoon as she had been doing for the past week, since Kunti had left the hospital.

Kunti was much stronger now, and during her visits they would chat as of old, whiling away the hours pleasantly. If she saw Kunti in the morning, in the afternoon she could keep an eye on Chandi Panday, who was back again at the market, selling until darkness fell. She felt responsible for Chandi and worried about her, although she now seemed less vulnerable to the wear and tear of the marketplace. Still, Aunt Adee felt that she should keep an eye on her.

As she approached Kunti's home, she began to think longingly of the cup of tea awaiting her there. True, Kunti wasn't quite her usual self, she had aged so much recently, but then she'd had such a lot to put up with. Aunt Adee tutted to herself as she remembered the things Kunti had said about her daughter-in-law, after swearing her to silence. She said that she did not want Jagru to know, did not want him to be further upset.

She was about to knock on the door, when it was opened from the inside. It was Jagru. Aunt Adee blinked at him, dazzled by his suit and tie.

'Morning, morning,' she said to him, 'you ma up?'

Jagru indicated that she was in the sitting room. 'Glad that you're here so soon, Aunt Adee,' he said. 'You're such good company for her. I wish you'd agree to stay.' He'd grown to appreciate the warmth which lay under Aunt Adee's appearance. It was people like her who gave the lie to stories of racial unrest, which were always being promoted with deadly effect by unscrupulous politicians looking after their own interests.

'I need the open space, Jagru,' she said. 'Me feel lock up in houses.' She frowned, as if some bad memory had intruded.

'Well, I hope you'll change your mind one day. You'll always be welcome.'

She did not reply to this, but called after him as he walked down the stairs, 'Mind now, do some good things while you up there. You don't want to sit around and wait til they change their minds and put you to clean the streets again.'

A brief smile flickered on his face, but he could not allow himself any kind of levity. He meant to make amends for his past foolishness. He would bring to this position, for which he had worked so hard and paid so dearly, all the skills and resolve he could command. He would do things properly, now that he had at last been given a chance to influence decisions. He wasn't open to being corrupted and he would not allow anyone to think so. If people wanted to see him, they should do so through the proper channels. He did not know why Paul Bagat had been trying to reach him, but the man should make an appointment and not waylay him on the street and press grubby notes in his hand. Even if he had been so inclined, he could not have made the meeting for the time stated on the note. The man should talk to his secretary. He really should.

Aunt Adee stood on the verandah watching as Jagru drove away. Her words to Jagru had been intended as light-hearted, but she realised that there had been some fear behind them. She did not know why she should be afraid for Jagru, except that of late, he had suddenly seemed to remind her of her son, who had been a lucky boy until they shot him.

'Is not all luck,' Kunti said as they sat sipping their teas.

'Who woulda believe your little son would become a minister,' Aunt Adee mused. 'I remember him running around in short pants.'

'I don't really like him being a minister,' Kunti confessed. 'Me worry about him. Of course, he worries about me, too. But I not likely to fall down again.'

The two women thought about the matter in silence.

'I saw Chandi yesterday,' Kunti said, changing the subject.

Aunt Adee showed interest. 'Me remember she leave early. Said she going to take out an insurance policy.'

'Can she afford it?' Kunti sounded bewildered. 'She return some money to me. Said that Jagru sent it to her to pay for six months' rent. She say the rent was being looked after, that she returning most of it, and would use some.'

'She working very hard at the market,' Aunt Adee commented, 'making good money. I sure she thinking about providing for she children if, God forbid, anything happen to she.'

'Well, she a good woman, a good mother. She really trying she best, considering all that happen to she. Not like some I know,' said Kunti.

'So Radika na coming back?'

'I hear talk she leaving the country.'

★ ★ ★ ★

Jagru had taken to arriving at the Secretariat well before it actually came to life. It was, he was sure, something that would enhance his ministerial reputation. As he turned into the parking driveway, he saw someone standing, no crouching, near the section reserved for his car. It was Bagat. He frowned. Why couldn't he come to his office like everyone else, or, if it was a social call, drop in at his home? Still, he owed Paul some gratitude for alerting him to his mother's plight, although Ma still hadn't told him what she'd been doing at that office, and had been unusually evasive when he mentioned the matter.

He tried to put a cordial face, but there was a furtiveness about the way Bagat jumped up to greet him which rankled.

'Hello, Paul,' he said, his voice curt. 'I didn't forget your note, but I had other things to do.'

'We've got to meet,' Bagat said urgently.

'Why don't you come to the office?'

Bagat grabbed his hand. 'You don't understand. I can't come to the office or call you. It would be more evidence and there's already enough.'

Jagru was getting annoyed. 'I don't know what you're on about, Paul, but I'm a busy person now. I just can't dash out of my office like that without any notice.'

'Phone calls. Your phone line's tapped. Phone calls I made to Radika. I was just amusing myself. But people might think we were conspiring and that your wife was the go-between. There's something else too, something I picked up at one of the embassy parties.'

Jagru freed his wrist. 'And why exactly were you calling my wife?' He thought he understood now why his mother had gone to his old office.

Paul Bagat backed off. 'Listen, I didn't come to make trouble. I'm just trying to warn you. I want to help. I'm sorry for what's happened.'

Jagru glanced at his watch. It was almost eight o'clock. He could not afford to walk into his office even a minute late. 'I've got to go,' he said, hurrying away.

Bagat kept pace with him. 'I really wish you'd take my warning seriously.'

Jagru stopped walking, stilling an impulse to tell Bagat to leave him alone. A momentary glimpse of the times they had spent together flashed before him. His voice was kinder as he said, 'Look, I'll look into what you've told me, but I don't think you need bother about a few phone calls, whatever was said. They wouldn't have made me a minister if I was considered a security risk. And really, I do have to go now.'

Had he been as paranoid as Bagat when he'd been with the United Party? During the entire conversation, Paul had kept one hand over his face as if to hide his features from some prowling spy. He was sure that what his former colleague was suffering from was the need to confess. He felt no desire to offer him absolution. But he saw now that he had underestimated Radika's desire to lash out at him with whatever weapon she could find. It put their last conversation of a few days ago into clearer perspective.

Wanting to do what was right, he had pleaded with her. 'It's your house as well as mine. Bharka and little Bunny are my children as well, as yours. At least come back, until we can sort out the future.' He looked around the flat. 'This place isn't very nice.'

'It's nice enough,' she had replied. 'Don't think you can sweet-talk me into coming back, Jagru. I'm still young. I'll find someone easily. If I go stick up with you again and wait until I get old it'll be useless to leave then to find a new life.'

'But Radika, you know I won't stand in your way if it's a divorce you want.' In truth he wasn't so eager for that just yet. Not when he had just been made Minister, but he didn't voice the thought.

She had laughed. 'Divorce? No, I don't think so. Not just yet. In a little while, maybe, but when I'm good and ready. I'm afraid if your nice new friends don't like the position Mr Minister finds himself in, that's too bad.' She had flounced away after that, saying she couldn't waste more time as she had to visit the hairdresser.

But just how serious had her relationship with Bagat been, maybe still was? What had she and Bagat been saying on the phone? It was an unpleasant thought that the Secretariat would have tapes which might touch on his intimate life. He was no schoolboy. Of course, he knew that the phone had been tapped, was being tapped, but the thought still left a nasty taste.

A chorus of 'Good morning, Sir,' greeted him as he walked into the office.

'I see I'm late,' he replied to their greeting.

'Oh, no, Sir,' said one of the typists; 'it's eight o'clock. You're exactly on time.'

He shook his head. 'Still, it's not my usual time. I've got to do better than this.' He ended the chitchat swiftly. It was time to begin the day's work without further delay.

His first sight of the numerous folders, touching on policies and their implementation in various industries, had not daunted him, but rather had inspired him and made him eager to start. The possibilities had always been there, waiting for the right people to make them into reality. There were, indeed, many in official positions who had the knowledge and the skills to carry out the policies which would create an economy boasting more than bread and butter survival. There were many within his own staff who were loyal and dedicated. Why then were things so constantly being bungled? The problem could not be money. Funds were regularly coming in from outside sources, loans for the development of some project, purportedly to benefit the people. Why were the people not getting the benefit? Why were projects not being developed? Where was the money going? As he grappled with the files, he realised that the problem was far more complex than he had even imagined. He would have to tread warily and guard his tongue from making accusations which might involve high-ranking officials. The task ahead would require great diplomacy. He would have to impress his views on his bosses without them thinking that he was too clever, a man to be watched as a threat. He had quickly learnt to identify the A.D. James clique and its leader's arrogant assumption that he was the real power behind the scene. He would learn to live with that. After all, what difference did it make to the lot of the poor whether it was James or P M Rouche who controlled things? Rouche was still ailing. The whispers about his decline were now very open and Jagru had begun to wonder whether some of the rumours were not being circulated by James and his clique. It was James who had appointed him and James who was suddenly calling a number of meetings, ostensibly to discuss directives, but mainly, it seemed, to establish where real power lay. They didn't seem to have any other point. The Old Man had not been seen for a number of days. But before Jagru had time to think over the implications of this budding belief, the buzzer on his desk sounded. Even before he pressed the receiver's signal, he knew that it was James's secretary arranging yet another meeting.

★ ★ ★ ★

Asha tried to keep Manu's children close to her, as she prepared to check out at the immigration barriers. Manu had already left, taking the first plane he could get, leaving Asha to bring his children. His trial was still in progress and if the wrong people had suspected that he would not be coming back, his departure might well have been blocked. So he had taken little baggage, to give the impression that he was just on one of his regular business trips. Asha had readily agreed to this plan, although now she was finding the children's restlessness something of a trial. Bulu had remained behind, and even though the business of obtaining visas had been tedious rather than difficult — as she had always said — she still wished Bulu was coming with them. She had tried unsuccessfully to persuade him to come; she suspected it had to do with some girl he was seeing.

She sighed. She herself had no such strings. Fleetingly, she thought of Jagru. She shook her head. She should never have encouraged the situation in the first place. It had been partly her fault, allowing her sympathetic feelings towards him to appear to be more. This was another reason why she was not sorry that she was leaving. If she stayed, she was bound to run into Jagru sooner or later and the whole thing might start all over again.

She had joined the check-in line. Others quickly joined and she heard the rising choruses of 'goodbyes'. She called to Manu's two little boys to keep their places in the line. They were in high spirits at joining what they called the 'big plane' outside on the tarmac. As she waited she felt something pull at her hair and turned around to see a little boy held high in someone's arms, entangling his fingers around the strands of her hair.

'What are you trying to do, you gorgeous thing?' she playfully admonished, as she tried to untangle her hair.

The woman who held the child was facing away, talking to a young girl next to her. She turned quickly at the sound of Asha's voice.

'Bunny, don't...' the woman broke off in mid command.

'It's Radika, isn't it?' Asha said coolly, as she finally managed to extricate her hair.

'Asha!' Radika blurted out, 'What are you doing here?'

'Same as you, I imagine. Leaving.' Asha turned away to call sharply to the two boys to keep by her. So Radika had indeed left him, as Jagru had said, and was leaving the country too. It didn't matter to her. It really didn't.

Radika picked up the threads of the conversation. 'I didn't know you were leaving. I didn't expect *you* to leave.'

Asha lifted her eyebrows. 'I didn't know we had discussed it.'

'I didn't mean anything. I mean... I thought, I guessed...'

The line was beginning to move. Asha wished it would move more quickly. She gave rein to her impatience in order to suppress another kind of feeling which was threatening to surface at the thought of going away. She had left before. She was, after all, a frequent traveller. But this was permanent. She was cutting her ties. She brushed the sentiment aside before it could overwhelm her.

Radika was making an attempt to reengage her in conversation.

'Not your children,' she said, indicating the two boys.

'My brother's,' Asha said. Radika knew very well whose children they were, but Asha tried to keep her voice friendly. After all, they were not rivals, had never been, as Radika no doubt supposed. She fingered the bracelet Jagru had given her, wishing that she had not worn it.

The line was now moving quickly and Asha moved along with it, burying her thoughts.

* * * *

Another week went by quickly for Jagru. When he was not involved in working on drafts and reports, he found himself in attendance at sudden meetings called by James. These continued to seem useless and taxed his patience, but after a while he adjusted, realising that they were part of the tradition at this higher level of the Secretariat.

The full schedule also helped him to forget. Occasionally, he recalled the way her eyes had laughed, her smile, but then by renewed concentration on his work he would banish the memory as if it were forbidden fruit. He was determined to forget, and his last ignominious moments with her helped. But it was difficult. Had she already left? She must have done. He had caught a glimpse of Bulu when he had allowed himself the luxury of driving past their house. But of her he had seen nothing.

She had gone, but his mother was still there. He was always grateful for that. He made a point of spending as much time with her as possible, feeling that her recovery from illness was a reprieve granted him.

Radika he had not seen since their last confrontation. He had received a garbled message from her that she was on her way out of the country. He concluded that she must have been making these preparations a long time ago, behind his back.

A.D. James did not like to be kept waiting and often sent his secretary ahead to the conference room to ensure that the others were already there before he left his office. Such had been the substitute symbols of power. Now his power was real. Rouche had been dead for several days now, though nobody knew that except he and his two most trusted men, Falder and Rook, and the two doctors who had attended the Old Man.

They had used these days carefully to prepare the way for James's assumption of the PM's role. He had moved with speed and certainty, and, in their secret council of three, his move for leadership had gone unchallenged. He had made both men his deputies, splitting the post, and this had seemingly satisfied their desire for power. Now they were confident that the takeover would be smooth and without controversy. James was not overconfident. There would be a few problems, but they had made damned sure that they weren't going to come from the Secretariat. For this reason he had ordered that the public investigation be intensified and the trials of Gordon Brown and Carl Blair be brought forward. They made plans, too, to stage a few more arrests to keep the public spotlight on their efforts to run a clean administration. After a decent period of mourning, he would even prepare the way to make Rouche fair game for criticism. The people would see that Rouche had been responsible for a lot of the bad decisions, as indeed he had.

He saw that everyone was present. Ministers, junior ministers and those who held the rank of ministers even though they were not given the title. He cleared his throat.

'Gentlemen,' he said, as he entered the room, 'please stand so that we can pay our last respects to our late Prime Minister.'

The gasps which came from some of them pleased him, as did the shocked surprise on almost all their faces. Had they really believed the old bastard was going to live for ever?

'I'm sure this announcement comes as a surprise to none of you,' he continued, breaking into the scant minute of silence. 'Our late and wise ruler, in order to effect a smooth transition to the new leadership, requested that news of his death should not be made public immediately. On his death bed, he counselled that this announcement be delayed even to you, his most trusted. Gentlemen, as the acting Prime Minister, I hereby declare a day of mourning. I also command your allegiance.'

No dissenting voice was raised. Jagru, sitting in the section reserved for junior ministers, understood with crystal clarity why Carl Blair, a possible dissenter, had been so quickly removed, discredited and placed on trial. The preparations for this morning's work had begun long ago.

* * * *

The figure was running away, stumbling as the bullet found its mark, changing the colour of the night to a bright unseemly red. Only it wasn't her son this time. Aunt Adee twisted and turned, feeling that she should recognise him. She awoke, convinced that she had been dreaming about Kunti's son. She sat up, hugging herself against the night's chill. She felt that there was some deep significance in this dream, a warning of danger. As soon as daylight came, she would hurry to Kunti's to tell her about it.

* * * *

In another part of the town, Chandi, too, was having trouble sleeping. She thrashed about in bed, trying to repel the dark, menacing shadows of her dreams. She awoke, badly frightened.

She made efforts to get hold of herself. She was on her bed, in her home, with her husband. Her husband? No, he wasn't there. She slipped off the bed and padded into the kitchen. But he was gone, had left even before the sun made the day bright. She tried to shake off a sense of foreboding. Nothing was wrong. Lal often left this early, kept irregular hours, had been doing so ever since he started mixing with his irregular company. She put on the kettle. A cup of tea would restore her.

★ ★ ★ ★

Lal Panday walked quickly down the road, enjoying communion with this, the darkest hour before dawn, feeling that this moment was akin to the state his party was in. They were in the dark hours now, but bright dawn would come for them, and with them light would flood the entire country. Happy days would come. So he absorbed the darkness, feeling that he had to understand it to see his path more clearly. It was good, too, to start the day early and to know that the old bandit, Rouche, was finally dead. They had to move quickly to take advantage of the news. There was some evidence that James had nothing like the same power base as Rouche. It was being whispered that there was dissension in the Secretariat. All this could be used to their advantage.

What was that? He glanced around sharply, sensing he was being followed, that someone was walking with great stealth behind him. But there was nothing, except the shadows of the night. He jeered at himself. Was he now getting afraid of the dark? All the same, he increased his pace and kept looking back, but there was nothing to see.

The first light was beginning appear over the horizon as he arrived at the party's rooms. He stopped under a lone street lamp to pick out the key he needed to open the door. They couldn't afford the extravagance of a watchman. He thought of the article he was going to prepare for the special newsletter they planned to distribute later that day. Quickly, he opened the door and was almost inside the building when he felt a sharp, piercing blow to his back.

    Even before he turned around, he knew that it was too late. The clatter of receding footsteps greeted his instinctive grasp after his assailant. He tried to pull the knife out but couldn't. The pain was overwhelming. He tottered backwards and fell to the ground. Somehow he avoided falling on the knife. He writhed and with all his remaining strength managed to pull it out. His blood gushed forth. With a similar effort, he pulled his shirt off and tied it around him, trying to stem the flow of blood. The pain was excruciating, but he was beginning to feel light-headed, chilled. He dragged himself towards the open door which was creaking to-and-fro in the wind. He slumped by the door, unable to move any further. As he lay there, slipping in and out of consciousness, his thoughts became fragmented. He had been going to write a speech. What had it been about? Chandi. She would be worried. He couldn't let her worry. He had promised her. But he might not have lived up to this. Had he made her worry? What had he done? He tried to trace the path of recent happenings, but it was all too hazy. How had he wronged Chandi? He felt an unquenchable need to reach out to her, to tell her that he had never meant to hurt her, to see her smiling at him, wanting to spend the rest of her life with him. He sank into unconsciousness.

★ ★ ★ ★

    The entire Secretariat seemed enshrouded in a web of suspicion. Jagru could not put his finger on what exactly was wrong, but the uneasy mood permeated even his own office.

He could see his staff exchanging nervous glances with each other and shifting their eyes away from his face when they spoke to him. Were James's plans not working out? Was he, too, going to rely on a regime of uncertainty and conflict? Jagru sat in his office, unable to work, waiting for the summons to yet another meeting. But no summons came. He perused the morning paper for news of what was happening. It was littered with eulogies for Rouche and congratulations to the new leader. A brief statement from James was carried on the front page. He was going to continue in the footsteps of his predecessor, to wipe out inefficiency from all sectors, even from his own office if it existed there. Mention was made of Carl Blair and Gordon Brown and the fact that there would be no leniency either for them or for others who had similarly failed in their duties. Jagru put the paper aside. So there were going to be more arrests. Would the intrigue never end?

He tried to carry on as usual, though he felt on edge. All sorts of movements were going on inside the Secretariat and within his own ministry. He was hampered, too, in his work by an inability to contact the people with whom he needed to liaise. They all seemed to be otherwise occupied.

The morning came to an eventual close. Jagru left, glad to be out of the atmosphere of uncertainty. In the car park he stood bemused. Where was his car? He had parked it as usual in the reserved space. He had not given any orders for it to be moved. He checked with security. They thought that the car might have been taken away for repair. He should check with Rook. Jagru walked slowly back towards Rook's office, beginning to feel alarmed. Why had Rook ordered his car to be taken away? Surely they didn't think that he was a threat. He had demonstrated his loyalty and commitment. Rook was one of the top three, whatever he did would come from the top.

He was told by the secretary to wait. Rook was busy, closeted with someone important. Jagru shrugged off the slight, not sure whether it had been intended. Half an hour went by in excruciating slowness, but still Rook did not emerge. The secretary seemed to have forgotten all about him and had disappeared through the side door. She returned about fifteen minutes later with a food box. She looked surprised to see him still there.

'Oh,' she said, 'I thought you'd gone.'

Jagru extended his hand wearily. 'I'm happy to wait.'

The secretary looked at him doubtfully. Jagru wondered whether this might be a good sign. She went into the inner office, telling him she was going 'to check'.

What exactly were they trying to do to him?

'Mr Rook is going to be busy for another hour,' she returned to tell him. 'He suggested you might be interested in seeing Mr Falder.'

Jagru got up. He was not exactly enamoured about being shuffled around in such a manner, but would it be better than waiting, or should he go off to lunch and then return to demand an audience with Rook? But he was not hungry and could not put off finding out whether there was any basis for his fears about his car's removal.

Tom Falder was in and would see him.

Jagru was relieved that there was no delay. He sank gratefully into one of the plush sofas in Falder's office. He narrated his story, beginning to feel that all his imaginings had been foolish, such was the other man's calm and friendly attitude.

'Rook must have knocked it up in some way, when he was driving in, you know, scrape the fender or give it a small dent. Perhaps he's trying to put it right as quickly as possible,' Falder suggested.

Of course, there had to be some such explanation, Jagru

thought. Why had he thought there had been anything sinister about the affair? He was getting paranoid.

The two men chatted for a moment. Jagru agreed that now James was in place, things would be better run. He trotted out the phrases the other man expected. Whether he was under scrutiny or not, it was as well to say the right things. The car would soon be back, Falder assured him, as they parted.

Jagru was glad to believe him but, back in his office, all his misgivings returned. The furtiveness thickening around him was unmistakable. How could Falder know that his car would soon be back? But then, why had Falder gone out of his way to reassure him?

Jagru was sweating now. He sat still for a while, then got up and began to pace the floor. Should he go and confront Rook, ask exactly what was going on? No, that was asking for trouble. Suppose it was all his own imagination? It wouldn't do him any good to imply that he felt under suspicion. He would keep calm. He had done nothing, had nothing to fear. He went back to his desk and began to work on some of the papers before him.

Another hour elapsed.

Then came the summons he had been half-expecting.

CHAPTER ELEVEN

They had chosen the conference room in which to grill him. He was not surprised to see that both Rook and Falder were present. They had an enormous folder and a tape recorder in front of them. Was it all about him? What had they concocted? And what exactly had Paul Bagat been saying on the phone to his wife?

'Ah Persaud, come in, man, come in. Have a seat.' It was Falder who spoke, still the same expansive, seemingly friendly person Jagru had spoken to earlier. So he was still going to play that part. Would Rook, then, play the hard-faced interrogator? Jagru took the seat indicated. The conference room seemed eerie, with only the three of them present. They were trying to intimidate him. Nonsense, he had nothing to fear. He was just being silly. It was no doubt just a routine matter of ministers reaffirming their loyalty because of the change at the top.

'I'm sorry it had to come to this,' Falder said, 'I still can't believe you're not innocent.'

'Shit, man!' Rook said coldly. 'We have overwhelming evidence against him.' He turned to Jagru. 'Just do us all a favour and don't waste our time denying it.'

'I don't know what you're talking about,' Jagru managed.

'I have orders from the PM, based on the evidence in this,' Rook tapped the folder before him, 'to strip you of your ministerial rank and have you placed under immediate arrest.'

'But a lot of it's circumstantial, isn't it,' argued Falder. 'It's going to be difficult to prove everything. I mean let's suppose he confesses to some of the minor things you've got on him, what kind of bargaining position would that put him in? A short sentence? Early release?'

Jagru listened in growing horror. 'I'm not going to confess to anything. I haven't done anything.'

Falder turned to look at him mild surprise. 'But the evidence is all there,' he said regretfully.

'But you said you thought I was innocent.'

'It isn't what I think, man. It isn't what I think,' said Falder, making his voice sad.

'Look, you're wasting our time,' Rook snarled. Perhaps a few nights behind bars might help you remember.'

'At least, tell me what I'm supposed to have done.'

Falder opened the folder. Photographs of Chandi at the marketplace and her daughter, Artie, standing in front of the shack. One showed him entering the shack with Aunt Adee next to him. Another showed him entering Chandi's new home. They had several of him with Asha. Good God! One of his wife and Paul Bagat, laughing together in a restaurant. Another showed him with Paul, who was trying to hide his face with his hand.

He pushed the photographs away in disgust. What did they reveal — except that they had gone to enormous trouble to pry into his private life? But that was not all they had. There were tapes, Rook was quick to inform him. They had begun to realise quite some time ago that his apparent defection to their side had all been a sham. He had never ceased working for the United Party. His wife had been the go-between. They had telephone conversations which proved that. But his activities had a far wider orbit than the work he did for his old party. He had been plotting to undermine and to discredit those who worked for the good of the country. He'd conspired with Lal Panday and others of the Worker's Party who'd been plotting to bring down the legitimate Government by force of arms. He had even conspired with Carl Blair. They held tapes of his conversations with Blair which were irrefutable proof of his subversive activities. He could not deny it.

They played some of the tapes to him. Jagru listened in growing bewilderment. His voice and Bagat's voice, but the conversations had never taken place. They had evidently spliced the tapes, and crudely at that.

'Those are faked,' Jagru protested. 'Anyone could tell that.'

'It's all right for you to say that,' said Falder, 'but you can see how much easier things would be if you did confess. You don't have to confess to everything. A confession that you've been working undercover for the United Party would do.'

Jagru saw things clearly now. They were looking for a scapegoat. James wanted to start his reign in a blaze of good opinion. How long ago had they planned this?

'I'm not going to confess to anything. You know I'm innocent.' Then he shut up suddenly, wondering if even these words could be misconstrued.

As Rook began the formal speech stripping him of his ministerial position, Jagru became aware that a man in army uniform was standing at the door.

'You're under arrest,' Rook ended.

Jagru was aware of the room suddenly being filled with people. Flashbulbs popped in his face.

He was taken to a police station about thirty miles outside the capital, the distance adding to his alarm. Not greatly to his surprise, his demands for a lawyer were met with curt refusal. They were not really holding him in custody. All he was required to do was make a statement, a written statement and then he would be released on bail.

Jagru knew enough to realise that writing anything would seal his fate. He wanted a lawyer present. Eventually, he was told that someone would be contacted for him, but that he would be kept at the station until then.

They took him down to the cells. Jagru cringed inwardly as they approached a large cell containing a number of desperate-looking men. To his relief, he was placed on his own in a small cell opposite.

This could not be happening to him.

He watched with concern as a young boy was pushed into the cell opposite. The youth immediately caught the attention of a huge man who must have been all of six feet and weighed about three hundred pounds. Jagru knew enough of what was rumoured to go on in the country's jails to be alarmed. How it started he did not know, but it was not long before the man was savagely cuffing the youth, who was ineffectually trying to defend himself. The other men in the cell had surrounded the two and were urging the big man to teach the boy a lesson.

Jagru shouted out loudly to attract the attention of one a police officer. Eventually an officer arrived, took one look at what was occurring and quickly opened the cell to drag out the boy, who by this time was bleeding from his nose and face.

'I'm innocent,' the boy shouted through his swollen lips. 'I'm innocent. Me just standing there, minding my own business. Me din do nothing. You ent got no right to lock me up.'

'He start it,' the big man muttered, as the officer led the

youth away. Then he called across to Jagru. 'Is you turn baby, you turn soon.' He skewered a twisting middle finger at him. 'Me gon split you ass open when me get hold of you. Man, you gon love it. You a virgin? You na know what you been missing.'

Jagru felt sick at the picture the man's words conjured up. He was glad that it was not just a cell, but the width of the corridor which separated them. They were like animals in a cage, the men across from him. How they had come to be so perverted and sadistic, so merciless in their dealings with their fellow human beings he would not speculate. Whatever, they had no right to walk with the civilised and their place was rightfully behind bars. But how could one support a system which so callously exposed a young and innocent boy to the likes of such savages. But at least these men did not hide what they were, unlike the men in suits and ties who sat behind their desks and inflicted suffering on the masses in order to feed their egos — and their bank balances. They were animals too, but in disguise, predators who ripped out the guts of their fellow creature's dreams. Now they were trying to scapegoat him with their crimes, to whitewash themselves and win a new lease to fool another generation.

He had followed what he thought were noble precepts all his life, striven to better the lot of his fellow human beings. This had meant more to him than even the good opinion of his friends, shaping his decision to join the treacherous quicksand which the Secretariat had proved to be. What had he done but to follow his dreams, urged along by the staunch principles he had been taught by his mother, who believed it was blessed to work for the good of others? His mother. He tried to shut out the images his despair conjured up of her pain and misery. He couldn't really believe that they would keep their promise to send word to her or bring him a lawyer.

He began to resign himself to the belief that they were going to keep him there for the night.

Movement in the corridor. Food for the prisoners. He refused his portion although he was extremely hungry. He could not eat. Too many things plagued him.

After a while, he dozed off. Some hours later, he jumped up with a start, momentarily fooled into believing that he was home in his bed, safe. The rough floor of the cell soon disabused him. His watch told him it was almost morning. He sat brooding in the darkness, listening to the rumble of his empty stomach and trying hard not think of how his mother would be worrying.

* * * *

For Kunti, too, morning came with painful slowness. Now at last she could find out what they were doing to her son. When she had seen Bagat at her door, she had wanted to shut it in his face, but he had quickly wedged his foot in.

'Please, please listen,' he had begged.

Kunti did not have the energy to feel as self-righteous as she had done when the incident was still fresh in her mind. If he was really sorry about what he had done, if he had come to apologise... But she kept him standing at the door.

Bagat had stood there awkwardly, a man who had something terrible to impart and did not known how to do it.

'They've arrested your son,' he said baldly.

Kunti stared at him blankly. What was he saying? When she understood that he was serious, her head began to swing and she stumbled back inside to seek the support of a chair.

Bagat followed her, concerned that the old woman would fall down again. He cursed himself for his part in the affair, the telephone calls — the foolish whim for revenge. But he *had* tried to warn Jagru, after the disclosure made to him by a drunken Tom Falder at an embassy party. Jagru had not wanted to listen, but Bagat still felt a terrible sense of responsibility. What part had he played in Jagru's downfall? The news had been on the radio. The new PM himself had made the announcement, declaring that even if his own ministers were guilty, they would be shown no quarter.

'Where they keeping him?' Kunti asked.

He didn't know. They would no doubt let her know in their own good time. Time to soften Jagru up, though he did not say this to Kunti. He watched her warily. He did not know how to leave, did not know if he could in good conscience leave her on her own. Her revulsion towards him seemed to have disappeared, faced with her son's troubles. He felt relieved in her acceptance of his presence, feeling that the burden on his shoulders had grown lighter.

They sat in silence together, but he could guess the fears passing through her mind. He wished she would say something. He could not think of anything helpful to say.

He got up. 'I'm going to see if I can find out anything.'

Kunti looked at him eagerly, 'You'll come back and tell me, son.'

Paul nodded. He did not trust himself to speak.

An hour later he was back. He had gleaned nothing, but he thought it would help if he outlined the efforts he had taken and the friends he had contacted in his search.

She grasped at his words, trying to find some solace. He sat with her for a while, before he left, reassuring her that he would return in the morning.

★ ★ ★ ★

They had taken him out of the cell. He was now sitting on a hard bench in the outer section of the station. He gratefully accepted the cup of coffee offered. His skin itched and his clothes were saturated with stale sweat and dust. He badly wanted a bath, but was afraid to make any request, even to enquire whether they had sent a message to his mother.

He had just finished his coffee when he realised that he was under scrutiny. An obese man, with 'official from James' written all over him, beamed at him with what were crudely meant to be taken as good intentions. The man stretched out his hand.

'Burrowes,' he said, 'Sach Burrowes, but I think we've met before.'

Had they? Jagru stared at the man. The memory jumped out at him. Of course, he'd met him before. Burrowes had been one of those who had given evidence against Tyler. He thought he had read something about the man being the main witness against Carl Blair, too, but he wasn't sure about this. Was Burrowes gathering material to repeat his performance as star witness for *his* prosecution.

Jagru eyed him with distrust.

'Is time we talk, don't you think?' Burrowes said.

'I want a lawyer.' Jagru had decided that this was all he was going to say.

'Be sensible, man,' Burrowes said. 'Let we talk this over. You'd like to go home and have a nice bath, wouldn't you, and forget all 'bout this?'

Jagru kept silent. He thought of his mother, of how distressed she would be. Perhaps if he gave Burrowes a little, they would at least let her know where he was.

'What do you want me to do?'

'Why you don't eat some food first. Breakfast, eh?' Burrowes encouraged.

Jagru found it hard to refuse. He grabbed at the food when it came, hurriedly swallowing it down.

'Will I get back my ministerial role?' he demanded after he had finished.

Burrowes shrugged his shoulders. 'You know that's impossible. Look at the evidence we got. It's all been on the news, man. Everybody knows what you done.'

'When am I going to get a lawyer?' Jagru asked again.

'Come, let's be sensible,' Burrowes said, 'you know there's no need for anybody to come, much less a lawyer. All you have to do is co-operate. You know how much lawyers cost. All this can be over sooner than you think if you're sensible.'

'What do you want?'

'It's very simple. All we want is an admission that your party was responsible for killing Lal Panday. We're not asking you to say you were personally involved or anything like that. Just that you knew they were making plans and that they intended the blame to fall our party, maybe even on Mr James.'

Jagru reeled. Killing of Lal Panday? He remembered the last time he had seen the him. Dead. How could it be? He thought of Chandi. Since the incident, he had not seen her, although he had sent some money, knowing it could not repair the damage he had caused, but hoping it would help in some way.

'Lal Panday! I didn't even know... I didn't even know he was dead!'

'I'm not asking that you should have knowledge of that. Just that you say you knew your people were planning to kill him.'

'You know this is nonsense,' Jagru said. He might as well admit to the murder as admit to conspiracy. It would be just as damning. They must take him for a fool. He would say nothing. They were just trying to trap him. The evidence they had on him was clearly not enough. They were so crude.

Burrowes got up. 'You'll be sorry,' he said. Jagru watched him go.

Later that morning, the message came they would soon be moving him to the Central Jail. His heart sank, and the despair that threatened to overwhelm was staved off only by the sight of his mother arriving with a group of people. Aunt Adee was with her and a man who looked like a lawyer. And there was Paul Bagat. Jagru frowned, thinking how they had accused him of collaborating with Bagat. What would they think when they saw him here now? He pushed aside the thought. He was tired of their games. He would not do their thinking for them. Still, he felt a vast relief to see his mother there. He had been afraid that she would not be able to withstand the shock of his arrest. Her face was drawn and haggard, but apart from that she looked well enough. He tried to compose his face, to erase the effects of the last twenty-four hours. People who cared about him knew what was happening. He was going to get a lawyer. Things would be put straight. It was going to be all right.

He had been in the Central Jail for a week now, trying to hold onto his courage, pinning his hopes on his lawyer's bid to use *habeas corpus* to get him released from custody, since no charges had yet been laid against him. He languished in the temporary section of the prison, reserved for those not yet tried, spending his days waiting for reports from the lawyer on the legal tangles which surfaced daily to postpone his release. He supposed he should be grateful for the tenuous distinction which kept him from being placed in the main lock-up. Sometimes, he heard screams after the lights went off. He tried to cover his ears, not wanting to be made privy to such cries. In comparison he had little to complain about, though he had come to suffer regular humiliations at the hands of one of his jailers, a sadist who rejoiced in the nickname of Dawg. Dawg derived much fun from carrying out body searches, poking about his private parts in a quest for unspecified, concealed objects. These searches were often made after he'd had a visitor, as if they suspected him of being aided and abetted in some plan to escape.

Jagru learnt not to protest after the first time, although he tried to hint at what was happening to his lawyer. But such was his lawyer's lack of success, Jagru began to wonder if he, too, was acting for the Secretariat. He said less and less to him. At the same time, Dawg encouraged him to believe that they were only toying with him, that the unnamed horrors of the night awaited.

'You gon like it when the time come. You gon get down on you knees and beg fo' more. See, you already got the taste,' Dawg told him as Jagru squirmed, trying to minimise the pain of the probing stick which the jailer had pushed up inside his anus.

Jagru tried to remain strong through the slow, cruel passing of the days and the attentions of jailer Dawg. He channelled his feelings towards his mother, worrying incessantly about her even though she came often and looked at first to be holding up to her ordeal well. She was often accompanied by Paul, whose evident concern for her began to revive some of Jagru's old feelings of warmth towards his former friend. Paul, though, was brusque and embarrassed when Jagru tried to express his gratitude.

Kunti, for her part, seemed to lean more and more on Paul

for support, bewildered by what was happening to her son. She had been optimistic at first that the authorities would soon realise that it was all a mistake and her son would soon be free. As the weeks and then months went by, she began to realise that they intended to keep him locked up for as long as they cared. Why did they not put him on trial or release him on bail? Why were they torturing a mother's heart in this fashion? As the strain told on her, she began to show signs of confusion. At times she behaved as if she thought her dead husband was still alive, speaking to him as if he were by her side.

And despite his efforts to reassure his mother that all would be well, Jagru's own resolve was dwindling as it became apparent that his lawyer, for all his activity, was getting nowhere. Increasingly he found it hard to imagine any end to his incarceration. His financial resources were also dwindling. The money in the bank had gone. His house and the land from his grandmother were both now mortgaged. He would be penniless by the time they were finished with him. He was on his own. There was no political party or organisation behind him to absorb any of the legal costs.

The months passed. He had lost count of how long he had been held. His visitors became increasingly concerned by how vague and disoriented he often seemed. But then the idea came to him that they were keeping him isolated, not merely because he had not been convicted, but rather because they were trying to break his spirit. This conviction saved him. He would not allow them to break him. Now he took a grim pride in refusing the blandishments of the smartly-suited men who came, satellites of Burrowes, hinting that there would still be a reprieve if he changed his mind.

He knew now that if he yielded, there would be nothing left between him and madness. He tried to condition his mind to accept his isolation, to make the walls of his captivity work for him. He began to think of God, to draw some energy from communion with a higher force. He prayed for understanding, for an inner light which would make him remain strong despite the circumstances, that would help him to remain true to himself and his beliefs. Sometimes, he thought of Lal Panday who had died for his convictions. They had trodden different roads, but in the end they had striven for the same thing. There were lessons to be learnt from what had happened to both of them. It was all too easy to see why so many were just content to continue their weary way, carrying the burden of plunderings of their rulers. Thinking about the daily sufferings of the masses, Jagru reflected that his own were small.

Such thoughts sustained and maintained his balance when he might have given in to his emotional pain, imagining himself lashed by long whips or stoned by crowds who had condemned him without wanting to know why and were bent on crucifying him.

One day, Ban came to visit him. He was wary, not knowing what to expect of her, not sure if this might not be another trick of Burrowes.

Her party was taking up his cause, she told him. The false accusations they were making about Lal's murder were ridiculous. Lal was a martyr, and a martyr he would remain in the people's minds, despite their rulers' efforts to surround his death with petty intrigue and conspiracy. In the end, they would be no more successful in besmirching the other political parties; they bungled everything else they turned their hands to. She told Jagru about the flowering of the students' movement for freedom in China. Her party was monitoring its progress closely and reporting it in their newsletter. The courage of the students was sure to inspire their own young people.

Jagru listened woodenly. Dawg was present because of what he termed the political nature of the visit. When he had to respond, Jagru's answers were non-committal. There was no point in provoking Dawg's malice.

Ban finally left, repeating that she and her party would continue to agitate for his release. Jagru listened doubtfully, not sure whether this might not be doing more harm than good, but then, these days, he was sure about very little.

'They gon pick up that woman again soon. Time she spend another spell in prison, though it don't seem to make no impression on her,' Dawg said sourly after she had gone.

Jagru said nothing. He knew that Ban had been constantly in and out of prison; it certainly seemed to have had little effect on her iron constitution. He wished he could say the same for himself.

Later the same day, he had another visitor. He hardly recognised her. She had grown much thinner and her face looked haunted.

'Chandi,' he greeted, pushing his hands through the bars. The embarrassment of their last meeting now seemed unimportant and he was glad to see her, eager to express his good wishes, his hopes that everything was going well for her and her children.

Chandi brushed aside his words. 'I wanted to see you,' she said, 'to tell you that I don't believe any of what they're saying, the way they're trying to make out that you had a hand in Lal's death. I don't believe any of that. I wanted you to know that.'

'I didn't. You know I didn't...'

Chandi stopped him. 'You don't have to tell me that. I have known you as a good man. I know you're still a good man, no matter what anyone says.' She averted her face: 'I want you to know, too, that what happened at the house is forgotten. I know what it is to go through life suffering because you feel you've hurt others or have been wrongly accused, and I don't want you to think that it still matters.'

At the time, Jagru knew he should have gone back to apologise to her, but he had shirked it, afraid of encountering an enraged Lal Panday. Now the words gushed out: 'I'm sorry, Chandi, I really am.'

She raised her hand. It didn't matter anymore. All was well and she wanted him to know that. She had needed to come to see him. He had done too much for her family for her not to pay this final debt, to make sure he had not been left feeling guilty. Lal might have thought evil things about the help he had given, but she knew he had done it simply out of kindness. She got up to leave, feeling that she could no longer look at the emaciated face, the hollow eyes which seemed more dead than alive.

'I've got to go back to the market. It's a busy time,' she said.

'Thanks for coming,' Jagru said gratefully, feeling that the visit had healed some part of him.

Was there anything he needed? Her eldest daughter, Artie, had been looking in on his mother, keeping an eye on her, but if there was anything he himself needed... Jagru shook his head, not trusting himself to speak as the time came for him to be taken back to his small cell.

Dawg came to visit soon after. 'Me din' know you so friendly with Lal Panday's widow,' he said, jabbing Jagru in the ribs. 'Eh-eh, perhaps there's another reason why you kill he...'

Jagru stared at him dully, not allowing the rage boiling inside him to surface, fearful of reprisals.

'Yes, that *would* sound convincing in court,' mused Dawg, 'but we'll stick to the original one. Don't want to lose our pet political prisoner, do we?'

Later, Jagru found out that Chandi's visit had been a way of saying goodbye to him. The next he heard of her was that she was dead.

It was Aunt Adee who told him. 'She had insurance, you know, on she life. After Lal gone, she broke down. She love she children so much, but it was the best answer, na, the only way to give them the better things in life. What a joke on the insurance company, ha-ha.'

Chandi had met a fatal accident on the way to work one morning. Jagru remembered her words to him, how she had taken time to come to reassure him that she did not blame him for anything, forgiving him for his momentary lapse of control.

'She children going to be all right, now,' Aunt Adee said. 'The big boy, the one who go way to sea. He back. He going to the college. Artie going back to school too.' She cackled: 'The insurance company going to pay up. They na can prove anything.'

Jagru wanted to cry, but he felt dry, empty, his tears used up. How did one change things in a society where suicide could seem such a rational and positive choice? His way? Lal's way? The way of the smuggler who used the system for his own ends? The way of his old party which went along, playing its part, waiting for the opening that would never come? The way of the masses, seemingly conditioned to accept their lot, just wanting to survive however they could, not wanting to know beyond that. What could one do? The days went by and he searched for new ways to look at the question, trying to forget his own situation, not that Dawg ever allowed him to do so. He had recently taken to visiting him at night to allow him the pleasure of listening to the BBC broadcasts on the collapse of the students' movement in China. Now that the students were on the run, Dawg came to gloat, glorying in the reports of the army's butchery.

'Let this be a lesson to you an you like,' Dawg warned. 'And you friend, Ban. They who play with fire, get burn! They killing them by the thousands! Thousands!' he guffawed. 'They din know when they well off. They had food in they bellies. Now because of they damn foolishness, they get shoot down like pigs.'

Jagru could not bear to listen anymore. Were the seekers of freedom and justice always to be denied? Would they always have to pay with their lives when those with power had forgotten the meaning of humanity? He did not know. He had suffered too much. He was beyond caring.

CHAPTER TWELVE

When they eventually released him, Jagru was more surprised than anything else. He had been imprisoned for over a year, had stopped expecting any favours and had almost become inured to Dawg's attentions. The release came without any fanfare. He could not understand it. They suddenly seemed to have lost all interest in him, as if he was yesterday's news. There was no more talk of trial, no more talk of signing confessions. Nothing. The door was opened and he was told that he could go. He had the dubious satisfaction of witnessing the stupefied expression on Dawg's face as he was given his release papers. Dawg, at least, would not be able to harm him any more.

His lawyer was jubilant. Jagru did not grudge him the credit and thanked him for his support.

'I came here straightaway,' the lawyer told him, 'when I heard that they were finally going to release you without pressing any charges. Of course, you might have a case against the state for false imprisonment, but you would probably be wise not to pursue it. Too damn expensive.'

Jagru nodded passively. No, he would not pursue anything. He was well aware that he could not pursue anything. He gulped in the free air greedily as he emerged from the prison. He was going to need to get used to it all over again, to renew his perceptions of this outer world.

He refused the offer of a ride from the lawyer. He would

savour the freedom to span the miles again. The lawyer protested — nasty accidents could still happen — and eventually, he prevailed upon Jagru to accept a ride to the market from where it would be easier to get transport home. He should go straight to see his mother, she would be overjoyed to see him — and lie low for a bit. He would be wise not to go walking around on his own for a while.

As he was about to get into the car, Jagru heard his name. He knew at once who was calling him, who would be interested enough to know that he had been freed. Maybe he had her to thank for his release?

Ban smiled at him. 'Looks like we finally defeated their propaganda machine, stopped them spewing out all those lies about your so-called crimes.' She got straight to the point. 'Are you going to join us? We need someone like you.'

Jagru shook his head.

'Take your time. Think about it. Don't let the thought of prison deter you. It's a prison outside too. I just came out of prison myself on another of their trumped up charges. You'll understand more what it's all about now that you've been in prison, yourself.'

Jagru shook his head again. He needed time to think, to get back in touch with himself and find out what he wanted. He did not know if he had any energy left to pursue universal causes. What was important was his mother. She had suffered too much already on his behalf. He was grateful that he still had her. Perhaps, if he did anything to expose her to further suffering, she might be taken away from him. He could not risk that. He would have to sit down and think about what was important and what was not and whose way was best. Perhaps God would guide him in his path, but at present his mind was confused.

'No,' he said to Ban, 'It's too soon. I need time to think.'

Ban said: 'Yes, think about it. You might change your mind. I hope you will. We'll be waiting.'

Jagru watched her drive away, trying to shut out her words. At the moment, all he wanted to do was to just walk along, feeling the healing qualities of the sunshine, the simple wonder of being a free man.

After the lawyer dropped him at the marketplace, Jagru stood and watched the crowd jostling for transport, hunting for scarce foodstuffs. For them, tomorrow was always there, always the next day. They had to make one day join another. They couldn't just forget the tomorrow that stretched inevitably before them, however uninviting it was, to fight for a different and distant tomorrow which might never come.

He found himself moving towards the stall where Aunt Adee bartered her plastic bags.

She jumped down from the stall with the agility of a young girl. 'Jagru,' she said, 'you out, boy! You out! They na get you after all. Every time we ask, they said next day, they going to let you go tomorrow. Son, this a one tomorrow we can celebrate.' She shook her plastic bags in a sort of jig and the deep rusty laughter welled up from inside her, even as the tears fell on her cheeks.

Celebrate? Could he really do that? Wasn't it just another day? What difference did his release make to the sufferings of the poor? Who cared?

'Does your Ma know?'

Jagru shook his head. He was going home now.

'Come on, come on. What we waiting for?' She took his hand and he allowed himself to be led. He became aware that children were staring at them and giggling. Two freaks, he thought. Two more mad people to join the crowd. He began to laugh himself, almost without pause, strengthening the impression of his wild appearance.

People moved aside to let them pass, their stares not lasting long, accepting the curiosities of the street as they were now conditioned to do.

Jagru had given of his best, drained all his inner resources to create a different tomorrow. Would it ever come?

He continued to laugh and Aunt Adee joined him, thinking that his laughter as a free man was a happy sound.

Narmala Shewcharan was born in Guyana in 1958, to third generation rice-farming descendants of Indian immigrants. After leaving school she worked as a journalist on the Guyana *Chronicle* and later worked as a senior reporter on a newspaper in the Turks and Caicos Islands. In the late 1980s she established a publishing company and founded a tourism magazine.

She came to the U.K. in 1989. She currently lives in Surrey with her husband. She is working on a second novel.